TAKING STOCK

The First Sixty Years

To: Karen on your birthday 7.11.05

May the oncoming year
be prayerful and have God's
hand on you always

David.

Also by Humphrey Clucas:

Poetry

Gods & Mortals (Peterloo Poets)
Unfashionable Song (Hippopotamus Press)

Translation

Versions of Catullus (Agenda Editions, re-issued by Hippopotamus Press)

Through Time and Place to Roam: Essays on A.E.Housman (Salzburg University Press)

Taking Stock

The First Sixty Years

by

Humphrey Clucas

The Lewin Press

First published in 2005 by The Lewin Press
19 Norman Road, Sutton, Surrey SM1 2TB

British Library Cataloguing in Publication Data
A catalogue record for this book is available from the British Library

ISBN 0-9550470-0-5

Typeset by Amolibros, Milverton, Somerset
This book production has been managed by Amolibros
Printed and bound by T J I Digital, Padstow, Cornwall, UK

CONTENTS

PREFACE

SOMETIMES I think that I have had four careers, at others that I have had no career at all, merely a series of jobs and hobbies – and hobbies that turned into jobs.

From1957 to 1961 my mother kept a journal. It is a fascinating record, not only for the period in question, but because the most important scenes of her life are done in flashback: my birth, my brother's adoption, her row with grandfather – tales which she told us so vividly that they came to have the quality of myth. I have hardly quoted from it; to the family, she can speak for herself. But it is clear that we share an instinct to preserve things.

I wrote my memoirs over about three and a half years (2000-2003), in the intervals of writing music. I began with an account of the very public sacking of Martin Neary, Organist and Master of the Choristers of Westminster Abbey. It was a highly charged period of my life, and until I had written it up, I could not put it behind me. I wrote as though for publication; I tried to be fair and moderate, I kept certain characters anonymous, and I included no fact of which I could not be certain. I called it *Interesting Times: Westminster Abbey and the Great Neary Scandal*, and in this form it achieved a modest circulation, mainly among cathedral musicians.

When I came to write the rest of the book, I was faced with what I think of as the Trevor Beeson problem. Beeson's two books, *A Dean's Diary* and *A Window in Westminster*, were about his time as Dean of Winchester and (earlier) as a Canon of Westminster. Roughly speaking, I was singing in Winchester while he was at Westminster, and vice versa, but I knew many of the cast of characters. He is waspish, and highly entertaining. But I could not write about my ex-colleagues as he had about his if I wanted any of them to speak to me again. There was also the possibility of libel. If I were to continue in the same way, therefore, there were clearly things which I could not mention. So I changed the rules; this was to be a private book, and I would say what I liked – because it was more fun. This unexpurgated version exists in an edition of four, two of which are held by my children.

Finally, I decided that I could after all make the thing publishable. The principal changes are two: I cut down the *Interesting Times* material and integrated it into the main narrative, and I removed the second half (the uncles and aunts section) from the chapter called *More Family*. It contained some rather startling information, about which I felt strongly; it also involved a sort of literary detective story. But it was not for the world's eyes, and would have upset the living, so it had to go. Apart from this, I softened, without essentially altering, some of my judgements (the line between charity and honesty is rather a fine one), and I removed some salacious and potentially damaging gossip.

Life has moved on since I began. One or two people have died, for instance, and poor Barry Brunton has disappeared. I have watched Brian Lara's second Test Match record innings – and so on. But I have mostly not updated; it would have been a continuous process.

I have said that I write to preserve things, but I also

implied that I do so to try to make sense of them. I do not know that I have succeeded. Nor do I know who my ideal reader is – possibly a literate and musical grandchild. My single grandchild is three months old. Well, I have cast my bread upon the waters.

January, 2005

One

FAMILY

IT WAS at a school called Liverpool College that the upwardly-mobile Clucas girls met the decayed-gentry Hough sisters and formed connections which were to last their lifetime.

My father's family were Lancastrian agricultural. John Lewin Clucas, my great grandfather, owned a seed shop in Liverpool, subsequently moving to Ormskirk; he is thus credited with starting the family firm, in 1860. He was a patient man, with high standards. But it was his son Archie, my father's father, who got things moving. Archie was the second son, and not the favourite. My Aunt Mary told me that his mother, a hard lady, did not hug him enough – "not that they went in for hugging much in Lancashire," she said, "in those days." Archie somehow acquired a small field, and began breeding his own seeds, discovering by instinct (my father told me) what scientists researched more formally later. By a mixture of genius and drive, he turned a small seed shop into a small international business with a Royal Appointment.

His wife Ann (no 'e' – "plain Ann", she would say) was the daughter of a slow and solid Lancashire farmer. She was pretty solid herself. She became a primary school teacher, but when she married Archie, she gave that up to help him; for years she kept the firm's books. She also, after a brief period in which he forgot to give her any housekeeping, looked after their personal money, doling him out (at any rate to start with) small sums week by week while she managed the rest. My father was devoted to her, as she was to him; she was of the generation who thought that sons were more important than daughters.

Archie had the defects of his qualities – chiefly a furious temper, which those close to him had to live with. "That all passed off very nicely," Grandmother would say, meaning that we had got through whatever occasion it was without Archie losing his temper. He also had sudden bursts of generosity; he once, quite out of the blue, gave me a bicycle – though it was my brother Stuart who really needed one.

Father had a difficult time with Archie. He was apparently taught to drive by being taken to Blackpool and then told to drive home. (He was always a terrible driver.) He was expected to join the firm; there was no question of anything else. When he was about twenty-one, Archie took over a failing business called Blatchfords; Father was sent to Coventry to run it. He was never praised and often criticised. He several times thought of quitting, but was dissuaded by his mother. After Archie's funeral, Grandmother told me, "He was a keen man at his business" – which seemed to leave a lot unsaid. My mother always thought that he had a mean mouth.

Any family money which we now possess is due in the first place to Archie, or perhaps to both of them; they were a self-made couple. They had three children: my father, christened Thomas but never known as anything but Tom, and two daughters, Mary and Lilian.

My mother's father, Joseph, or Joe, was a dentist, a dear, gentle man who never made any money. Her mother, Clara, was the strong one. She was small, with clear eyes and a straight back; she loved us all, but one knew where one stood. For years, they took in lodgers to make ends meet. Clara's own father, a sea-captain, had died on board ship, aged forty-four; her elder brother Otis, still in his teens, had to go out to work to keep his widowed mother and his five brothers and sisters. Otis later became an architect. I remember him in old age; he insisted on living alone in a remote part of Wales, where he would have heart attacks half way up mountains. Visiting him in hospital once, my mother was told, "I'm *so* glad it's you, Theo; such a *plain* lot of women come in here." (This in a loud voice; he was deaf.)

Another relation, Aunt Bella, was psychic; she would have extraordinary insights when hypnotised. My mother inherited her gift, but never used it because my father did not like it. A session at the Ouija board once produced the sentence, "Man in glasses go away"; this was Father. Anyone less psychic I can hardly imagine. My mother and her sister once visited a fortune-teller who immediately sensed my mother's powers, and was staggered that she was not using them – as though she had inherited a fortune and refused to spend it.

Joe and Clara were intellectually curious; having tried various forms of Christianity, they finished up as Unitarians. ("Oh, Unitarians!" said my Uncle Graham; "they don't believe in anything much except kindness to animals." He was given to sweeping statements.) They had three children: Graham, the eldest, Theo, my mother, and Carmen. My mother was christened Theodate. Insofar as this was spoken at all, it was pronounced as a sort of fruit (three syllables), rather than in the Greek way; but in fact she was never called anything but Theo.

The Hough sisters used to visit the Clucases during the school holidays. My father, who was a little older, was not part of this society. "Really," he said once, "when a lot of girls get together, you can hardly hear yourself think." Later, he changed his tune. He had to propose to my mother twice; she turned him down the first time. Years later, someone remarked that "Tom still looks as if he can't quite believe Theo accepted him."

They were married in Ormskirk Parish Church in 1934. Archie had wanted a big wedding; he was a big man in Ormskirk by this time, and was soon to become Mayor. But my mother knew her own mind, and had also learned how to stand up to Archie. They announced the date of their wedding – and then quietly got married the day before, with only a handful of family present. "Tom must have known that I was peculiar when I married him," Mother said to me, not long before she died. They began their married life at Birchenholt Farm, outside Ormskirk, within sight of Archie and Annie's new grand house, Red Trees. They had a live-in maid, to whom they paid ten shillings a week and her keep, which sounds like exploitation, but was in fact the going rate. They were young, and enjoyed themselves. Mother remembered Father returning to Birchenholt late at night with some rugger-playing friends, and waking her up because they needed a fourth at poker. Father told me that he once danced all night (he was a very poor dancer) and went to work the next day without having slept at all.

The problems of the inter-war years do not seem to have impinged very much. Mother was in Austria just before war broke out; she was advised to go home, but does not seem to have been particularly worried. An earlier visit to Vienna had been the occasion of a rather notable dinner party. Mother and Father had invited some business acquaintances called Frankl; at the last minute Mother decided to include Egon, an old Austrian boyfriend. She was, after all, married, and she thought it would be nice to see him again. ("Are you a good girl, Theo?" he had apparently asked her. "Yes," she replied, "unfortunately I am." Girls didn't in those days.)

The evening was a disaster. The Frankls looked down on Egon because they were wealthy and he was a poor medical student; Egon looked down on the Frankls because he was Aryan and they were Jewish. Father was jealous of Egon because he was an old flame of Mother's; Egon was jealous of Father because Father had married his girl. Alas. It was the Frankls' son, Ernest, who, re-inventing himself as an Englishman, eventually married my mother's sister, Carmen, and became Senior Tutor of Trinity Hall, Cambridge.

My mother lost her first baby, after which she almost died, of thrombosis and other complications. She was never as strong again. For the last twenty years of her life she lived on an unlikely diet consisting of a few things she knew she could digest. Ever since I became conscious, I had known about her afternoon rests, though I only discovered the reason for them when I read her journal after her death. Her mother had brought her up not to make a fuss about illness.

It was this illness which finally brought my father closer to Clara, his mother-in-law. When he was still engaged, he once concluded an attempt at conversation with the phrase, "normal, ordinary people like us". "Normal we may be," she replied, "ordinary we are *not*."

Poor man. Now, however, they were united in a common cause. They became very fond of each other. It was easy to be fond of Joe.

Mother was desperate for another baby – anything in a nappy would do – and as soon as possible they adopted Martin. For my mother, he entirely replaced the son she had lost, and Father wanted anything that Mother wanted. We all knew from an early age that Martin was adopted, and so did he, but it was never an issue.

It was an issue for Archie, however; he did not see why his money should go to some stranger's child. Mother eventually told him what she thought of this, and there was a sharp exchange of views. Within a few hours, Archie had climbed down. Neither Mother nor Martin had any further trouble with him.

I was born on November 16th, 1941, in Lancaster Royal Infirmary. It was the worst time of the war. Uncle Graham was a prisoner of the Japanese. Mother and Martin had moved to live with her parents in Cartmel; my father worked in Ormskirk during the week, and could only join them at week-ends. He was also in the Home Guard. Archie had rather unscrupulously retired so that Father, as head of the firm, would be kept at home on necessary war work. After the war, he came out of retirement again.

In due course my brother Stuart was born, on June 14th, 1943; there were five of us. In 1945 we moved to our house in Formby.

Two

EARLY LIFE

I SUPPOSE I am lucky to have been born at all. After my mother lost her first baby, the doctors would not allow her to conceive for a considerable time. When they finally gave the all-clear, my poor father, who had nearly lost his wife once, was so appalled that he could do nothing at all to initiate my conception, and it was only when this psychological barrier was removed that I became possible. (Perhaps my children are similarly lucky; I had mumps six months after I was married.)

I was born by Caesarean section. When my mother's first child was still-born, she was so ill that the doctors would not allow her to be told. It was only when her own mother, an unconvincing liar, said to her, "The doctor told me to tell you that the baby is being taken care of in the other room," that she knew that she had no baby. All this is most movingly described in her journal. The account of my birth which follows is a slightly different version which she sent to me on my fiftieth birthday:

> I remember so clearly my first waking moments after your birth; hearing the Ward Sister saying, "You've got a little boy, Mrs. Clucas," and myself

> saying in a dull flat voice, "They told me that last time." Then seeing her shocked face and hearing her horrified voice saying, "What!" Thinking I had not spoken clearly enough, I repeated in a louder voice, "They told me that I had a little boy last time."
>
> Then I suppose I must have gone off again for a short while, for the next thing I remember was seeing Sister standing by my bed with a little bundle in her arms. Then she laid your small warm face against my cheek, and held you there for a brief while, and then, at last, I really believed that it was true.

I still cannot read this, or the much longer journal version, without emotion.

I was christened in Cartmel Priory; the vicar, Lawrence Dykes, my mother told me, was wearing corduroy trousers. Fifty-six years later I happened to mention this to the current organist of the Priory, Adrian Self. "Yes, that sounds like old Lawrence," he said; "he only died last year." Old Lawrence was descended from John Bacchus Dykes, the Victorian hymn composer.

My earliest memory is of standing by my bedroom door in a blue dressing gown and saying, "I'm three-and-a-half and nearly four". I also remember going downstairs with my father (both of us in dressing gowns) to listen to the news; the war was still on. These memories are of our house in Formby, called Cartmel Lodge; I do not remember the house in Cartmel. When I was told that we had won the war, I could not understand who 'we' were: my mother, me, Martin?

I ought to have had a happy childhood, and in many ways I did. I was loved and cared for, and we had no financial worries. If I was not always happy, perhaps the fault was mine – or perhaps it was no one's. I was thin-skinned, and in my earliest years had a temper. Except in certain musical matters, I did not strike out on my own. I was always looking for the role models, the self-elected leaders, wanting to be part of the in-crowd, hoping to do the right thing. It did not help that I was small for my age, and my voice broke late. This basic insecurity stayed with me for a long time; it was not until I was approaching forty, for instance, that I felt I could say what I liked in a staff meeting.

(Though I must have been confident once. When I was still in my pram, a rather silly neighbour tried to woo me. "Oh, Humphrey," she said, "couldn't you call me Auntie Dodo?" "No, Mrs. Palmer," I replied, "I couldn't." Years later, a gushing acquaintance approached Tristram, our younger son, outside the Queen Elizabeth Hall. "What's your name, my little man?" she asked him. "Tristram," he replied gruffly, not giving an inch. "And how old are you?" "Seven." After which he pointedly stood about twenty yards away until we could get rid of her. I think we both showed sound judgement.)

Our life at home followed a steady pattern. Father went out to work five and a half days a week, and slept on Saturday afternoons. Mother ran the house and looked after Father; she changed her dress in the evenings. She was helped to start with by a series of maids who came and went ("Where are the maids?" I once asked, from my high chair), and latterly by Alice, a hard-working and provident Lancashire lady of no social graces, who was eventually able to buy a small house, cash down, from what she made working for Mother, potato-picking, and so on. She dressed out of jumble sales, and listened to the radio in the dark to save electricity. As to the social graces, she once brought in a joint to a dinner party with the announcement, "If that there's too bloody for yer, turn it over on t'other side." To start with, she lived in; later, she came daily, and Stuart took over her bedroom.

Cartmel Lodge itself was a large family house on three floors, with an acre of grounds. The road was unadopted, which meant that the council did not look after it, and was on the wrong side of the railway line. It was untarmaced; we filled in the inevitable holes with cinders. Apart from an army barracks, there was little between us and Formby shore, about two miles away. The railway ran between Liverpool and Southport; trains passed every quarter of an hour, but after living there for a month or so, we ceased to notice. The grounds were looked after by a full-time gardener. For years this was Mr. Todd, a sour and dour man whom none of us ever became fond of; later we had Albert, who was rather a dear. I think that they were paid by the firm; it was felt that a seedsman's garden was an important piece of advertising.

There was a front path with beds on either side, and a small sunken garden; a front lawn (later a tennis court); a small spinney; a back lawn, and a rose garden with a summer house; a vegetable garden; and behind all that again, a small field, actually the property of a neighbour, in which we practised cricket and football. (It was too small; we used to lose the ball.) The vegetable garden held potatoes, peas, runner beans, broad beans, red currants, black currants and strawberries (beneath those nets which did not really keep the birds out). Nothing since has tasted quite so good as roast lamb with mint sauce, peas and new potatoes, the mint and vegetables straight from the garden. I also enjoyed climbing trees (I once terrified my maternal grandfather doing this in Formby woods). One tree, 'my' tree, became so familiar that I could be at the top of it within seconds. (Stuart also had 'his' tree, a sprawling and inferior affair.)

Vegetables were my father's delight; nothing made him so happy, he said, as a healthy field of cabbages. It was his pride to produce new potatoes for his birthday – May 29th. On holiday with my mother, in Italy, say, he would prod and poke at what he considered their rather poor vegetables, with no intention of buying them. This embarrassed my mother, who would walk away. He would continue to grow things into extreme old age – though someone else had to do the weeding.

I was naturally thrown into the company of my younger brother, Stuart (known as Gussy, from his initials – G.S.). Martin was nearly five years older; he was always leaving schools before I got to them, and though he treated us with great kindness, referred to us as 'the little boys'. He was good at all sports, not particularly intellectual (he failed all his 'A' levels), and – I am moving on a few years – always seemed to have a girl friend, which was a thing I found hard to acquire. There was a whole series of these. The first was called Jean Cairns; we have a photograph of them in tennis gear at our house, aged about seventeen. Much later, she became his second wife. His first wife, Virginia, is also in the picture. I think he got on with Stuart better than with me; it was only towards the end of his life that we became closer.

Stuart was eighteen months younger. He was lively, amusing, inventive and slightly scatty; people noticed him. He could find ways of entertaining himself which would never have occurred to me. There is a studio photograph of us, aged perhaps six and four, in which Stuart is playing with something and I am watching him; possibly this is typical. He was also prone to small disasters. Given a chocolate Easter egg, he decided to break into it by taking a golf shot at it with a small baseball bat. For weeks afterwards we were finding bits of chocolate behind the furniture. Years later, after I was married, he decided to demonstrate the unbreakability of an orange squash bottle by dropping it on our kitchen floor; of course it broke. "It could have happened to anyone," he said – but it tended to happen to Gussy. Because he was so amusing, I think we sometimes did not take him seriously enough. He also, perhaps even more than I, looked very young for a long time; Martin, on the other hand, grew up fast, and as a teenager looked older than he was. Partly for this reason, I think that Martin was allowed to do more, sooner, than we were. There is also a tendency – certainly my mother suffered from it – to baby the youngest one. (I began to go grey in my late twenties, and from the age of about forty have looked considerably more ancient than I actually am. I have had the worst of both worlds.)

I must also mention family holidays. These began, in a modest way, just after the war. Two of the earliest were at Deganwy, near Llandudno. There was a public swimming pool, which held a swimming gala – races, diving, and so on. There were also clown divers. "The same dive," they would shout (the same, that is, as the serious diver's) and leap off the board in various grotesque fashions. Gussy and I thought this was wonderful, and had to be taken several times. We also had successful holidays at the Raven Hall Hotel in Ravenscar, near Scarborough. This offered not only tennis courts, a putting green, clock golf, bowls, a swimming pool and a nine-hole golf course, but also a 'host', a young man who arranged all sorts of competitions and tournaments, some of them fairly light-hearted. (At Novelty Putting I did the first hole in one – blindfold.) There was dancing in the evening, and a weekly cricket match against the village. We also arranged our fortnight to coincide with the Scarborough Cricket Festival; Mother and I, in particular, were devoted cricket watchers. (More of this anon.) Gussy and I were quite young the first time, but later we went as teenagers.

Happening to be in the area in 1992, Janet and I dropped in for a drink; it was all still going on.

We also had some good holidays in Jersey (Father tended to nip across to Guernsey to look at tomatoes). Our penultimate holiday was in Le Lavendou, in the south of France. A Pernod before lunch made one delightfully sleepy afterwards – a new experience. I have a photograph of myself in Jersey, aged eighteen, with each arm round an attractive young lady, all of us in swimming costumes – though I do not remember that I got very far with either of them.

Tennis, the beach, swimming, dancing, a little (a very little) sight-seeing – this was the pattern. Mother loved the beach, and the sun, though she had given up playing tennis after her early illness. Father did not like the beach at all; he was too fair-skinned, and he could not swim, but he cheerfully put up with it because we liked it. He was the most generous of fathers. He was also concerned that Gussy and I should be able to swim, and when we did not seem to pick this up naturally, arranged for us to have lessons. For a small, plump man, he was surprisingly good at tennis, or at any rate surprisingly active. He was not particularly fast and had no style whatever, but he could keep going for long periods, apparently without a hair out of place. Mother said that he used to emerge from rugger scrums looking much the same. He continued to play doubles on our court at home until they left for Essex, when he was fifty-seven.

Our very last holiday, in 1962, was in Ischia. Martin had dropped out of this sort of thing several years ago, and I was already at University, but Gussy and I came willingly enough; it seemed too good to miss. We were shown round Pompeii by some business friends of Father's, two young men in their thirties. We had lunch with their elderly parents, who lived in Naples. Thirty-five years later, I read my mother's journal. In 1959, Mother and Father had been in Italy on business, and Mother had clearly fallen rather heavily for one of the young men, and he (at any rate temporarily) for her. He was twenty-nine, she was forty-eight. 'The sinister thing is,' she wrote, 'it catches you unawares. You deceive yourself by pretending that they are little curly-headed boys who appeal to your maternal instinct, and by the time you realise that it isn't your maternal instinct at all, it is too late.' Alas. I am fairly sure why we had a last family holiday, after a gap of a year, in that particular part of Europe.

A word about dancing. Dancing classes were held in Formby village hall, run by a dancing school from Southport. They were great social occasions for the local youth. We learnt quicksteps, waltzes, foxtrots, sambas, and country dances like the Dashing White Sergeant and Gay Gordons. These latter, along with the much more complicated Eightsome Reel which I learnt later, have rather passed from my memory, but I still enjoy a very occasional waltz or quickstep when the chance arises. At one time I used to make a point of dancing with Penny Neary on choir tours – any sort of music would do. I once did a waltz with Jill Scott, Charles Brett's sister, on a cross-channel ferry, to *Stanford in C Nunc*. I am not very good at it, but occasionally my partners were; dancing with a Welsh civil servant on a hotel terrace in Turkey suddenly became very easy. (On another hotel terrace, in Yugoslavia, Janet was being whirled round by the Succentor of St Edmundsbury Cathedral. A *grand dame* in our party leaned across to me: "Hammersmith Palais," she said.) Janet is indulgent about my dancing; she says I have rhythm in my head but not in my feet. The most surprising people dance well; one of her best holiday partners was sixty, queer, and shaped like a pop bottle.

At the age of four, I was sent to the infant end of the

local prep school, called Holmwood. It was two or three hundred yards down the road. I can remember little about it except that I was taught by a nice, fair girl called Miss Bailey and an older, darker lady called Miss Whitmore. The atmosphere was gentle. There were coal fires in the classrooms in winter. I was taught piano by Miss Dunn, who wore long, flowing garments and had slightly grand airs. My piano lessons were more than once interrupted by a Mr. Cox, from the main school. Even at that age I was aware of something slightly charged in the atmosphere; I think a rather hopeless flirtation was going on. She was much older than he was.

Holmwood was the scene of my first musical triumph. Dressed in a white surplice, with angel wings attached, and aged just five, I sang the first verse of *Away in a manger* at a Christmas concert. My poor parents, who had not been forewarned, were quite overcome. I had not bothered to tell them; it did not seem very important. I always knew I could sing.

It was also at Holmwood that I first met Edward Craig. He lived just round the corner. His parents were quiet and retiring, and they doted on him; he was an only child. His old grandfather, who lived with them, spoke fairly broad Lancashire, as did Edward when I first knew him. Grandfather was also rather deaf. Having heard on the radio that Mozart was born in Salzburg, he came out into the garden in some excitement. "Edward," he said, "did you know that Mozart was born in Southport?" After Holmwood, I rather lost touch with Edward until we were both Public School boys, by which time the Lancashire accent had gone. He was a tolerable pianist, and as teenagers we made, and listened to, much music together. I also bowled to him for hours in the net in his garden; we played cricket for Formby schoolboys. I shall say more about him in the 'Cricket' chapter, with an account of how he and my cousin Liz changed the course of cricket history.

When I was eight, I went to Charney Hall Preparatory School in Grange-over-Sands, and from that time on was only at home in the school holidays. I am not sure why my parents thought that boarding was a good idea. Certainly, it would have been done with the best of intentions. I know that Father wanted us to go to a good Public School, and I suppose that this was the preparation; but I could have stayed at Holmwood, as Edward did.

I have no very strong feelings about Lancashire, certainly nothing like the sorts of feelings which Janet has for Devon and Cornwall. Partly this is the way I am made; I did not really feel I had begun to live until I was eighteen. When I was writing poetry, I did not seem to be able to draw on childhood for my themes, as others did. But I wonder whether my comparative lack of feeling for it is partly because from the age of eight until I left home and married, I was only actually in Lancashire for about one third of the year.

Charney Hall was not a very good school; I think it had been better. There were about sixty pupils when I got there, a hopelessly uneconomic number. It had been smaller; the annual cricket competition was called 'Sixes', dating from the time when four six-a-side teams were all that could be managed. The headmasters were Mr. Duncan and Mr. Hirst; the other two fixtures were Mr. Hopkins and Mr. Topham (Hoppy and Toppy). They were all Oxbridge men; Toppy, I think, had been a rowing blue.

Hoppy, who taught Latin and Greek, was extremely old; he celebrated his eightieth birthday while I was there. His standards of perfection were The Dragon School and Horris Hill, names which he repeated as mantras; we were never able to live up to his vision of how things were done there.

Martin told me years later that Toppy was a bottom-pincher, and rather keen on Mother. I knew him as the most boring teacher I ever had. He taught English and History. We read novels round the class – but that was all we did with them. They were never introduced, discussed, or made alive in any way. We also learnt twenty lines of poetry a week; we plodded through 'John Gilpin' in this way, and 'The Forsaken Merman'. There was no attempt to link this week's chunk to last week's, or indeed to discover any meaning in it at all; the repetition was the thing. I remember suddenly noticing that a few lines in 'The Forsaken Merman' (I have forgotten which) sounded rather nice – and that is the only pleasure I ever got from Toppy's English lessons. In History we read a text-book and answered questions, and once a term we learnt (again) the dates of the Kings and Queens of England. (Does anyone now remember the rhyme 'Willy, Willy, Harry, Ste,/ Harry, Dick, John, Harry Three…', etc., which at any rate gave one the sequence, if not the dates. Or all those rhymes in Kennedy's Shorter Latin Primer – altered by us to Kennedy's Shortbread Eating Primer: '*A,ab,absque, coram, de…*'; I do not remember what came next. There was also something rather important about 'towns, small islands, *domus* and *rus*'.)

Mr. Hirst, who taught French, lived out in the town, and thought he was rather a lad. (It is easy to show off to small boys). He had played rugger for Wasps.

It was Mr. Duncan, who lived in the school with his wife, who seemed like the real headmaster. He gave the impression of being a slightly disappointed man. I disappointed him even more. A few years previously the school had had a Winchester scholar; there had not been a public school scholar since, and Mr. Duncan had convinced himself that I would be the next. When I failed, he did not speak to me for several days. He taught Maths, and occasional Geography; somehow we were expected to know Geography without being taught it.

It was Mr. Duncan who gave an early blow to my confidence. Once a week, we had Mental Arithmetic; I was always quick at this, and I suppose I was able to answer first more often that not. One week he told me, "We've heard enough from you; it's time we heard from someone else." This was confusing. I had thought the point was to answer as quickly as possible; if one was not supposed to do this, what was one to do? Anxious for approval, I felt lost.

Apart from the rather variable teaching, the main way in which the school was poor was that we were left too much to ourselves. Of course we got up to various sorts of mischief; at one period there was some rather unpleasant bullying. But we also invented our own entertainment; there was a succession of crazes, of the sort that small boys have. For a while it was canasta, a card game which we played endlessly, and about which I can now remember nothing. Towards the end of my time it was roller-skating, at which we became extremely skilful; we even played volleyball on roller-skates.

There was a sequel. When I was about forty-five and a form master, I decided that my form would raise some money for charity, and imposed a Sponsored Spell. By the following year, they were thirteen or fourteen, a nice crowd who had found their feet and wanted to organise their own event; they decided on a Sponsored Skate. Some would skateboard, some would ice-skate with parents at the weekend, some would roller-skate. I was fairly sure that I could still roller-skate, and also that the idea of my doing so would seem unlikely enough to make some money. So I borrowed some roller-skates, had a little practice the night before, and completed my ten laps of the playground with much ease and enjoyment, wondering why I had not been doing this for the last thirty years. A local press photograph records the event; 'marketing the school' was the buzz-word of the moment.

I must not give the impression that Charney Hall was all bad. I enjoyed the sport, for instance. I was only a moderate sportsman, but in such a small school it was not difficult to get into the first eleven for one's last two years, both for cricket and football. Cricket I particularly enjoyed. We played most afternoons, and there were nets in which one could practise for hours. Matches against other schools assumed a huge importance. The whole school watched home matches, which must have been fairly boring for them, though I do not remember minding it myself; away matches meant car journeys and an adventure. The headmaster's mood depended on how we did. I can still remember the sense of belonging which I got from my last year's cricket team; the previous year had been less happy. Both, I suppose, taught me something.

By ourselves, we played a lot of table-tennis and snooker ("Proficiency at snooker – sign of a mis-spent youth," said my father), and towards the end of my time a tennis court became available. We arranged our own tournaments, aided by a fat and amiable master called Mr. McCulloch. This had to be done in the evenings; the official game was still cricket. For a fortnight, though, everything stopped for Sports. The climax of this was a race called the Hampsfell, a free-for-all from the top of a local beacon, perhaps two miles away, and finishing on the school field. The last section was along a narrow stony path on which no overtaking was possible; if you were ahead then, you were almost certain to win. In my first year, I won Throwing the Cricket Ball for my age group; I think I discovered sooner than others how to hold the ball. I never improved, and as an adult had a poor arm.

The school had its own miniature rifle range which we all used once a week, and a gymnasium, with wall-bars and a vaulting horse, where we roller-skated. For swimming, there were the local baths. When the grounds were unfit, we went for walks through the woods and fields, which I probably did not appreciate enough at the time. Toppy would take in great lungfuls, and declare, "Breathe the air! It's worth a guinea a mouthful!" We were an active lot.

We also read a great deal, or at any rate I did. There was a small library, with Standard Authors. I worked my way through John Buchan, and the Hornblower and Sherlock Holmes stories. There was a Reading Prize for the best list of books read during the year. I won this in my penultimate year; I failed to do so in my last year because the headmaster could not believe I had read so much. No doubt I skimmed.

And then there was the music. It could not be said to be a musical school in the sense that we now understand it; nevertheless, music was fostered and encouraged. The first music master I knew, Mr. Nicholson, soon left to be organist of Cartmel Priory; Mr. Baker, who followed him, a nice, gentle soul, and Mr. Fairclough, an odd little man to whom we did not really take, were successive organists of the local parish church. The only instrument on offer was the piano, but we all did class singing. *Songs from the Hebrides*, I remember ('Over the sea to Skye' was a particular favourite); also a Novello book containing such things as 'Where e'er you walk', 'On wings of song', and 'The lass with the delicate air'.

There was an annual music (i.e. piano-playing) competition, and a carol service at which I sang solos (one year I sang the wrong verse). I learnt bits of easy Chopin: the A major Prelude, and the first part of the F minor Nocturne (Op.55, no. 1) before it gets difficult; also the Brahms A flat waltz (all sixths – hard for small hands).

Musical Appreciation extended into our free time; we borrowed the records and played them on a wind-up gramophone. We almost wore out a Mozart piano sonata movement (I forget which); we also liked Sibelius' *Finlandia,* though we much preferred side two to side one.

A term or two behind me came a rather fat boy called Paul Kenyon, always known as Dan. (We called each other by surnames – I was Clucas Major; but 'Dan' was a nickname, and therefore quite different.) Dan was a splashy pianist, but far more fluent than I was, and he also introduced me to the idea of composing. What made him think of composing I do not know – his parents were not musical; but after a while several of us caught the bug, and writing things in manuscript books became a feature of our lives. Some time ago I still possessed a setting of Stevenson's 'Requiem', written when I was thirteen; it was a simple tune with a chordal accompaniment, correct enough though not very remarkable. Dan became organ scholar of a minor Oxford college (minor musically, I mean); I have not heard of him since.

I left Charney Hall in 1955. Happening to be in Grange-over-Sands thirty-odd years later, I went to find it. The school had closed down in the late 1960s, and was now the site of a housing estate. All I could recognise was a piece of wall. I still have the Shakespeare Head Press complete Shakespeare, given me as a leaving prize; it is signed 'W. Maxwell Duncan, M.A. (Oxon)'. I also have Stuart's leaving prize; things must have gone downhill by then, since he only got the Albatross Book of Verse.

In the mid-1960s I watched Lindsay Anderson's film *If* in a Bexhill cinema. There is a scene where a smaller boy is being beaten by prefects; they take a ten-yard run-up with their canes. The audience around me thought this was hilarious and unbelievable; to me it seemed like a not too gross parody of what actually went on.

Uppingham in 1955 was a hierarchical sort of place. One did not speak to people in the year above, while School Prefects, who wore straw boaters, and tail-coats on Sundays, were god-like figures and also figures of fear. (In my third year we had a rather poor House Captain who was almost a figure of fun – but he was the exception.) We lived in twelve boarding houses, about fifty boys to a house. Within the house, and to a large extent outside it, discipline was run by the boys – hence the prefects' beatings; however, boys could only beat with a gym shoe. There was also a fagging system; one was a fag for two years. Regular duties included cleaning the prefects' studies, shoes and corps kit. Other jobs were awarded by fag call; the cry of 'Fag!' would go up from the prefects' corridor, and the last to arrive was lumbered. Occasionally one could get away with sitting tight in one's study, but this was risky. As study fag for an American scholar, I was required to press his trousers; inexperienced at this, I scorched them, and was beaten.

There were all kinds of rules and regulations which had to be learnt. A certain patch of pavement could only be walked on by one house. Trouser pockets were stitched up; after nine terms you could open one pocket, but not put your hand in it. And so on. After a fortnight there was a test; among other things, we solemnly learnt the masters' nicknames. Had it been done with a lighter touch, it might have been positive; one would have felt included. But it was all pretty dour and unforgiving.

Then there was the CCF, the Combined Cadet Force, or Corps. This was in theory voluntary; in practice, one was handed a small piece of paper containing the question 'Do you wish to join the CCF?' and told to write 'Yes'. The Corps suited Uppingham very well. There were rigid hierarchies: lance corporal, corporal, under-officer. The advantage was that you could shout at people of lower rank than yourself and they had no right of reply. Corps always started with a House Inspection; this meant that we stood in rigid ranks in the House Quad while the senior men shouted at us – for not standing rigidly enough, for not cleaning our kit properly, or whatever. People who seemed quite reasonable during the week turned into screaming heads for two hours on a Friday. For a brief period I tried very hard; my shoes were shinier than anyone else's (uniform came later). But I soon learnt to hate it.

Towards the end of my time I made life difficult for my housemaster over the CCF – as over other matters. John Colville was a good man, and I was lucky to have him as a housemaster. He was a firm disciplinarian; I was briefly taught Maths by him, and it was no easy ride. But he, and his wife Barbara, were also modest, warm, unassuming, and had our welfare at heart. They came to all the (Church of England) chapel services, but were really Congregationalists, and worshipped in the town as well. They were teetotallers. Mother and Father took to them at once. The CCF problem was that towards the end of my time I decided that I was a pacifist. I did not actually ask to leave the Corps; I merely behaved as sloppily and unco-operatively as possible, and took to bringing anti-nuclear war pamphlets by Bertrand Russell on parade. Having somehow achieved the rank of lance corporal, I removed my stripe. John Colville's difficulty was that he himself had been a conscientious objector in the war. He dealt with it by suggesting that, though he respected my views, perhaps I was making life a little difficult for my house captain.

Looking back, I have the impression that there was not much room for non-conformism, but that I nevertheless managed to get away with quite a lot myself. Perhaps there was more room than I thought. The attitude of the boys was in many ways more rigid than that of the staff. When in my last year we were taken to the Royal Tournament and I expressed my dislike for this sort of thing, I was told a) that I ought not to hold this view, and b) that I did not really hold it at all, but was only pretending to in order to be different. On the other hand, when I claimed to be not only a pacifist but an atheist (Bertrand Russell's *Why I am not a Christian* was my text), I cannot remember any fuss being made about it by the staff. (Boys, however, stole my book, probably on the grounds that I ought not to have it.) I continued to sing in the Chapel choir, a contradiction which was not to resolve itself for about twenty years.

Academically, I was pretty idle, getting by on what I picked up in lessons and a moderate amount of native wit. Sometimes I was found out. My reports were not always good. I took 'O' levels at fifteen, passing in English Language and Literature, Elementary and Additional Maths, Latin, French and Scripture, and failing (quite unnecessarily) in History and German. Later I acquired 'A' levels in English and French, and failed History. I did Chemistry for one year; I can remember making salt, and not understanding the equations. This was the sum total of my Science teaching. I did Additional Maths in a set which was taught that if it did what it was told, we would pass without necessarily understanding it; this worked quite well.

Post 'O' level, I did a little more Maths, and came to a point where I could not follow it on any basis; clearly I had reached my limit.

Masters taught in gowns in those days, and carried mortar boards. Much of the teaching was of a good standard, and never worse than solid but dull. Mr. Belk was never dull. He seemed old to us, a bachelor, very shabbily dressed. At one time he owned a car, which the boys called 'God' because it moved in a mysterious way. He taught me for 'A' level History and English, if 'taught' was the word. There must have been lessons when we actually did the syllabus – *King Lear*, I can remember, and Book One of *Paradise Lost*; but mostly one got him talking about something else, or he did it of his own accord. We once had a whole double period on Egyptology – not planned, it just happened. He was particularly fond of Stuart; I have a second edition of *Winnie the Pooh*, initialled 'T.B.B.'26', and subsequently inscribed, 'To the smallest Clucas in hopes. T.B.Belk'.

For most of my time, there were no specialist English teachers; Mr. Belk was a historian, I think, and classicists and language teachers all taught a little English as well. It was only in my last two years that a pair of bright young men, Gordon Braddy and Brian Stokes, swept away the cobwebs of this old amateur tradition, and gave us a glimmering of what University English might be like.

The boys, as I say, were more rigid than the masters, but the whole system was self-supporting and virtually seamless. Games, for instance, were structured much as at Charney Hall; there were official school games—rugger, hockey, cricket, fives and running – and if you wanted to play football or tennis, you had to do it in your own time. Games were mostly taken by masters, but there was a schoolboy Captain of Games, with organisational duties and powers of punishment for misbehaviour or failure to attend. Martin was Captain of Games in his time; an excellent sportsman, he acquired school colours for rugger, cricket, running and hockey – the first time that this had been done. Father, as an ex-rugger player, had always wanted us to go to a rugger school, but I hated it. In my last year, on days when games were organised on a House basis, I would volunteer for nothing, find myself left over at the end, and announce that I would go on a run – and then not go. I usually went to the Music School instead.

The music staff seemed to be somehow outside the system, a gentler and more reasonable race of beings altogether. Uppingham has always had good music. Edward Thring, the Victorian headmaster who built it up from nothing, decided that there were no good musicians in England and applied to Germany. His greatest find was Paul David, son of Ferdinand David, who had given the first performance of Mendelssohn's Violin Concerto. Thring was a minor Victorian poet, and in due course produced a series of School Songs, with much of the music by David; we used to sing some of these at school concerts. We always did the School Song ('Ho, boys, ho!'), and often the Football Song. This was a rather imaginative *czardas*. In the slow section, three wizards in a cave, rather like the *Macbeth* witches, create a rugger ball ('Wax from murdered owners rive, / Sulphur smothered all alive, / Strip of hide of madden'd bull, / Breath of cobbler, fill it full.'). In the hectic fast section, the game is played. The best of the songs is 'The Return'. In 1876 typhoid struck Uppingham; with great daring, Thring re-opened the school at Borth, a remote Welsh village. He describes standing on the station platform wondering whether anyone would turn up; most did. 'The Return' is an unaccompanied part song about leaving Borth; it still seems to me quite moving. 'The Cricket Song' had rather ludicrous words: 'The wickets are set, the field is met, / O the royal game and free, / O the royal game and free. / The school (the school) shall win (shall win), / Short out (short out), long in (long in)…' And so on. This seems not to be in the book of School Songs which I still have, but I remember it vividly. We never did it. We always hoped to do 'Farewell, thou Noble Wood', since Wood was the name of the Director of Music, but we were never allowed to.

I have a copy of Thring's *Borth Lyrics* published by J. Hawthorn in 1881. Hawthorn's was a funny old bookshop which survived until well after my time. In Borth Centenary Year, 1977, Hawthorn's found some old copies of *Borth Lyrics* – which they sold at the original price. They did not have a clue. We used to go in and ask for left-handed biros, and striped ink.

Another good idea of Thring's was that each boy should have a study, a tiny space that he could call his own. A few of the original studies still survive.

To return to the music staff. Mr. Wood was of the solid but dull variety, though a good man in his way. He was keen on Handel oratorios; *Messiah, Samson, Semele* and *Judas Maccabaeus* were all done in my time, with the school choir and orchestra, and professional soloists. We also did *Dido and Aeneas* in my first term (a concert performance), and much later the Brahms *Requiem*. The latter was expensive, he told me, because you had to hire extra brass. We never did Bach, but I remember a Haydn Mass, and one year when we were at school over Easter we sang Charles Wood's *Mark Passion*.

Robin Wood gave me piano lessons for three years (he was taught by a pupil of Clara Schumann), before passing me over to Vivian Bean. His room contained a large photograph of Joachim, with the opening phrase of the Beethoven Violin Concerto in Joachim's own hand; Joachim had played the Beethoven at the opening of the new concert hall in 1902 (he was a friend of David's). It had a wonderful acoustic. The inscription over the door read *Caesorum comitum memores*, which we thought, or pretended we thought, meant 'Caesar commits to memory'. By my time the building was used as a gymnasium; now it is the school theatre.

Robin Wood put a lot of time into improving my sight-reading for the Choral Scholarship trials. Some of this we spent on the tenor clef, which was supposed to be a requirement. I have been asked to sing once from the tenor clef in the whole of the rest of my life.

Mr. Wood came to a slightly sticky end. After a sabbatical term, he found that the Chapel choir had been taken over by a much younger colleague, and that he was not to have it back. He resigned, and went to Malaya. Too many people saw him as dull. But he was certainly solid.

The most distinguished musician on the staff was probably Anthony Baines, who was an authority on old woodwind instruments, and who wrote what was then the standard book on woodwind. I once heard him play the serpent, and he taught more than one boy the ophicleide. But I had little to do with woodwind.

Apart from Robin Wood, the fixtures were Jill and Vivian Bean, and Jim Peschek. In my third year I thought I would take up the violin; Jill taught me, in the firm and direct fashion in which she taught everyone. I covered the early ground quite quickly. When we did the Brahms *Requiem* two years later, Jill told me I was to play the viola; the first movement has no violins. I never returned to the violin, and for a brief period was quite a competent viola player, though I did not own an instrument; I borrowed Vivian's. Jill was an excellent accompanist, in the sense that she could get through most things – Brahms Sonatas, for instance. There was a photograph of her in the Music School, leading the orchestra in 1947; she looked young, and very pretty. She was probably the only woman in the picture. She never left Uppingham, and died of cancer quite recently.

Vivian took over my piano lessons at a time when I seemed to have got stuck; he revived my interest. We would start with a chat about cricket, then play some two-piano music, and finally get down to work. He was a kind and gentle man. For a while he was acting Director of

Music, but it did not suit him. Years later I did a *Messiah* at Leatherhead School, and he was in the audience. We met once or twice after that – he was a good host – but he died soon afterwards. It appeared that he had had huge health problems since childhood, and was only kept going by a series of operations.

Vivian and Jill did what seemed to many an extraordinary thing. Though apparently quite contented, they suddenly announced that they were divorcing in order to marry two other people, and that Vivian was leaving Uppingham. Jill married Bill Pickering, who had taught me Chemistry. I do remember one of us (not me) telling Bill that Mrs. Bean was waiting for him at the bottom of the stairs, and him coming back looking pink. This was years before the divorce. Vivian married a nice lady called Helena, with whom he was living when I re-met him. After he died, she gave me his Grove's Dictionary, the 1900 edition. Bits of this are interesting; the article on S.S.Wesley, for instance, was clearly written by someone who had heard him play.

Jim Peschek in my time was the music department's bright young man; by the time my children got there, he was a mildly eccentric old fogey who had stepped down from being Director, and the bright young man was David Dunnett, now Organist of Norwich Cathedral.

Jim had been a Choral Scholar of King's College, Cambridge (he was the first to sing the tenor solo in Howells' *Coll. Reg. Nunc Dimittis)*, and it was he and Keith Ross who suggested that I ought to follow the same route. Coming from an unmusical family, I knew nothing about such things. Keith, one year older than I, had been a King's chorister and was determined to get back as an adult. Finding that there was not much future in his callow baritone, he turned himself, largely by will-power, into a very serviceable counter-tenor, who was to sing in cathedral choirs for much of the rest of his life. Jim taught us both. I do not think I learnt much about production, and perhaps he talked rather a lot, but he was very encouraging. Jim is still with us; he ought to have been dead several years ago, having had much of his liver destroyed by cancer. He is delightful. Keith and I were the first in what was to be a long line of Uppingham choral scholars.

Two Uppingham institutions, both of them still going, were the Uppingham and District Concert Club and the Paul David Society. I had imagined these as existing from time immemorial, but in fact they were both started by Douglas Guest, Director of Music in the late 1940s; later he became the rather ineffectual Organist and Master of the Choristers at Westminster Abbey. The Concert Club put on a series of professional concerts in the school hall, which were open to both school and town. In those days you could book the Birmingham Symphony Orchestra or the LSO for about £300. Paul Tortelier came once, accompanied by Ernest Lush. He played the Richard Strauss Sonata, and the Hindemith Variations on 'A frog, he would a-wooing go', reading the verse in his wonderfully eccentric English accent.

The Paul David Society, run by the boys, put on two or three chamber concerts a term. Keith and I once did the alto-tenor duet from the Bach *Magnificat*, with a small orchestra conducted by Anthony le Fleming. Anthony was the son of the composer Christopher le Fleming; he subsequently became a music adviser in Birmingham, and later in Devon. In my last year I arranged a concert of English music, including a trio of my own, and concluding with Constant Lambert's *Fear no more the heat o' the sun,* for soloists, choir and strings. Jim conducted. Later I sang the brief tenor solo again at Boris Ord's memorial service. In the mid-1980s there was an old boys' Paul David; I think it was the 250th. Jonathan, my elder son, and I sang a

Mendelssohn duet, with Jim accompanying; Jim had taught us both. Jill played for Peter Cropper in some Dvorak; he was already well known as leader of the Lindsay String Quartet, and was probably Jill's most distinguished pupil. He was an involved performer, and led her quite a dance. I remembered him as a very young music scholar.

The concert choir I have already mentioned. I also sang without a break in the Chapel choir (treble, alto, tenor). This was my first introduction to canticle settings by Stanford; *Dyson in D* was also a favourite. They were arranged with unison passages for the whole school at appropriate moments. I do not remember doing much Tudor music. I twice sang the treble solo at the end of the *Harwood in E flat Benedictus*, a surprisingly good piece which no one now seems to do. I also recall doing the (high baritone) solo in Howells' *A spotless rose*. Jim thought I sounded tired. I did not tell him that three of us had spent the whole afternoon discovering Byrd's Three-part Mass.

And then there were the competitions. The most amusing of these was the House Singing Competition. For this each house had to provide a unison song (known as the House Shout, in which everyone took part), and a part song. In my last year, greatly daring, I chose a TTBB part song, with myself on top; but we did not have a strong enough bottom bass.

The Crosthwaite Sonata Prize was for movements from duo sonatas, both parts played by boys. I accompanied a clarinettist in one of the Schumann *Fantasiestucke*, and in the first movement of the Saint-Saens sonata; a bassoonist in the Saint-Saens bassoon sonata; and a viola player in Gordon Jacob. (Even then the hierarchies held. The bassoon player was older than I; we made music together, but did not really speak.) In my last year I accompanied a violinist in the Elgar Sonata; a little later, the same gentleman played the first movement of the Beethoven concerto with the school orchestra. He was a good player, but is mainly memorable for his sex-change operation, after which he re-emerged as Claire.

I won the solo singing competitions twice as a treble and twice as a tenor. In the intervening year, with a barely broken voice, I came sixth. This was higher, however, than a terrific hearty called Moore, who thought he was quite a man. He was told that his voice was 'immature', which some of us found rather funny. In my tenor years I sang the pieces I had prepared for my choral scholarship trials: 'But thou didst not leave', from *Messiah*, and the *Benedictus* from the B Minor Mass.

The instrumental competitions were simultaneously for individuals and houses; points were awarded, and there was an overall house winner. My own house, Brooklands, were not a musical lot, but in my last year we lifted the cup, though only two of us really contributed; the other was Bruce Ogston, later to become a professional singer. I won the piano class with the Brahms G minor Rhapsody, much impressing John Warrack, the *Daily Telegraph* music critic, who adjudicated. I was second in the violin class, playing the York Bowen Viola Sonata; this was in my brief viola period. The highlight of my chamber music career was the last movement of the Brahms Clarinet Quintet; the other four players were all in the National Youth Orchestra. I have loved the piece ever since.

I also won the piano class in the previous year – but this caused a row. I played John Ireland's *The Island Spell*, which sounds more difficult than it is. Anthony le Fleming chose Chopin's F Minor Fantasy. He cannot have played it very well. When he only came third, he stormed out in a huff (the official explanation was illness), and Jill Bean had to take his place in the chamber music.

Of course this was all schoolboy stuff; my only real way forward musically was as a singer. (Eventually I became a composer – but that was much later.) Describing it now, however, makes me realise how lively and active it all was – and how hard I worked at it. Uppingham was repressive in my time, but not Philistine. Stuart, for instance, took part in school plays, but he also got a lot of value out of the Art School, finding the same sort of freedom as I had in the Music School. Art was initially taught by an old boy called Rissik, who did wishy-washy watercolours with a huge amount of sky at the top and a tiny bit of landscape at the bottom. But he was soon followed by Warwick Metcalfe, a vigorous new broom, who never left Uppingham, and is now a retired elder statesman.

I have said that I was not always happy at Uppingham; if it was partly their fault, it was also partly mine. 'Nothing, like something, happens anywhere,' says Larkin – and so does teenage rebellion. By the time my children reached Uppingham, much had changed. Fagging had gone, and so had prefects' beatings. The range of sports was much wider; Jonathan went sailing. He also, in his first year, called the house captain by his first name, and borrowed his squash racquet. Community service was an alternative to the CCF; Tristram gardened for an old lady. The whole atmosphere was lighter. I decided, rather comfortingly, that I had been ahead of my time.

Three

CAMBRIDGE

IT WAS at Cambridge that I began to feel like a real person, and that the lines of my future life were laid down. I went up as a callow youth, and emerged as some sort of musician; I acquired an English degree; and I became engaged to Janet.

As a member of King's choir, I found myself part of a small, ready-made society in which I could feel comfortable. Our musical life was centred on the chapel, and our social life revolved quite largely round each other; degree work was a sort of optional extra. The chapel services followed the standard cathedral pattern: two services on a Sunday, five week-day evensongs (one of them men only), and a day off. The difference, apart from the standard, was in the rehearsal time: we had an hour each day, from ten past four. This left twenty minutes for tea, which we took with a variety of hosts: the Dean, the Chaplain, old Schofield, who had been University Librarian and who had known A.E.Housman.

In 1960, David Willcocks had just taken over from Boris Ord. I have recordings, made in the 1930s-50s, of Boris's choir and others. The worst of the rest are fairly comic, the best just about respectable. Boris, however, was making a different sort of music altogether; he was clearly way ahead of his time. David, who had been his organ scholar, had come back to pick up the torch.

As I write, David is over eighty, and it is fashionable in some circles to run him down; orchestral players, for instance, apparently never liked him. But at the time he was a huge influence. He had rigorous standards, and only these would do. He was neurotic about tuning; leading notes and major thirds had to be exaggeratedly sharp, a habit which has stayed with me, and which has sometimes caused problems. He once told us that he would rather hear a Victoria motet (I think it was) played by a string quartet; they might tune it better. In the end, I thought, he would never hear anything in tune. His other bugbear was blend. His method was to cut out all the sounds he did not like ("Mr. X, you are making a noise like a lay clerk"); what was left was what he wanted.

Inaccuracy was unthinkable; one became a good sight-reader, or one spent time with the music. I was quick in those days, and by the end would back myself to read almost anything. I remember going to the first rehearsal of Graham Whettam's *Evening Canticles* (we did the premiere in Coventry Cathedral) deliberately not having looked at them. (Or perhaps this was only the *Nunc*.)

Sometimes he was brutal. "There's a nasty noise coming from somewhere over here," he would say, pointing directly at some hapless bass; or "There's a nasty noise coming from Cantoris tenors, and it isn't Mr. Taylor," which was equally precise. And once, memorably, "Mr. Y, you are the worst alto we have ever had here." (Messrs. X and Y both became professional singers.) One Christmas morning he kept us rehearsing far beyond the normal time, making me seriously late for lunch with my parents. No doubt we had partied too long the night before; but Christmas spirit meant little to David.

Somehow one did not mind any of this, or take it personally; it was clearly about the music, not oneself. He did not seem sufficiently interested in people for it to be personal. In years to come one would be greeted with great affability, for about thirty seconds; it took a really distinguished musician – Bob Tear, say – to keep him longer.

And of course he was not fierce all the time. Sometimes he was great fun; mostly, we just got on with it. But he was always a tense conductor; after I left, it took me several years to get my shoulders down.

We certainly made some memorable music. I shall not forget the second movement of the Brahms *Requiem* during a thunderstorm ('Behold, all flesh is as the grass' – we did it in English; 'albeit the Lord's word endureth for ever'...) Several years later I took Jonathan to hear this piece; he was two, and rather difficult, so we stood at the west end. He was spellbound. It was his first experience of King's, where he was later a chorister. Also memorable was 'By the waters of Babylon' done very quietly to an F minor chant by Garrett, on a dark winter's afternoon, with that dark panelling which has since disappeared. The later recording of this is unaccompanied, which is not the same thing. You could sing very quietly in King's; I left feeling that anyone who sang above *mezzo forte* was not really a gentleman.

We made some good recordings: the Handel *Coronation Anthems*, with Thurston Dart on a huge double-decker harpsichord; the Allegri *Miserere*, with Roy Goodman on the high C's; the Byrd Three and Four-part Masses, with the top line of the Three-part carried almost entirely by Charles Brett; a Taverner disc, with the first recordings of *Dum transisset* and the *Western Wynde* Mass. And carols, of course; we sang some of David's early carol arrangements from those purple banda-ed sheets, which smelt.

They have dated now, and even at the time seemed rather full of passing-notes. I slightly regretted, too, that he took to the carol industry quite so whole-heartedly, and with John Rutter; there seemed something second-rate about it. Perhaps he liked the money. I still feel, though, that his popular descants are better than any of their successors.

The organ scholar when I went up was Simon Preston. Simon then was much as he has been ever since: vibrant and demanding in rehearsal, an exciting player, and a somewhat restless personality ("Jeepers!"). He told jokes in a hyper-active manner; it was he who introduced me to the Kodaly joke ('Could I but express in song' – 'Kodaly: Buttocks-pressing Song'). He also had a repertoire of extremely foul limericks, one or two of which (alas) I still remember. Sometimes he clashed with David. I recall a processional hymn in which (David conducting) they each tried to impose their own speed; neither would give way, and neither won. He remained difficult, as those who knew him at Westminster Abbey will confirm. The Dean in my time, Michael Mayne, told me that his results there were achieved at some cost.

Simon was succeeded by John Langdon; for a year, they overlapped. John had been David's senior chorister at Worcester, and there seemed an element of favouritism in the appointment. He was a competent player, but a rather less good conductor. In my final year, just before Christmas, David was away for a week; standards slipped so badly that we sent him a round robin asking that Charles Brett be allowed to take rehearsals in his absence. He never replied. We could have had Steuart Bedford; I remember him as very tense at the auditions, but he went on to quite a distinguished career.

The other choral scholars in my year were Charles Brett (alto) and David Thomas and Peter Cairns (basses). Charles was a Wykehamist, with all the effortless superiority of the breed. He was a lovely singer in those days, and also a fine accompanist; we once did some Fauré together, and his marks are still in my copies. He gave the impression of not practising, though this cannot have been true. He did other things well, too – sport, for instance. He gave up wicket-keeping to preserve his hands, but had kept for Winchester Colts to Richard Jefferson, who eventually bowled rather briskly for both Cambridge and Surrey. And he beat us all at squash. On leaving Cambridge, he got a job at Eton by the simple expedient of going to see the Provost of King's, Noel Annan; King's and Eton are under the same foundation. Later, he became director of music at Westminster School, while continuing his solo career. Eventually, he pushed his luck too far; taking time off in the middle of term to sing opera in Germany is not something one can do too often. When I last met him, he had a new French wife, who looked about twenty-five. I have sung with his son, Francis, who is rather a good bass.

David Thomas was barely eighteen when he came up, very young and very brash. His leg was pulled considerably, which he took in good part. He made a fairly rough noise. Years later, Wilfred Mellers described him in the *TLS* as 'one of the truly great singers of eighteenth-century music' – but it still sounded like old Dave to me. He spent two years pretending to read architecture, but was never going to complete the portfolio. In his third year he was allowed to do Parts I of both Archaeology and Anthropology (one subject) and Egyptology, in an attempt to complete a degree; I believe he passed Egyptology. He would sit in the Copper Kettle and ogle a slim and beautiful Ugandan princess; later, he married a nurse, who looked quite like her. Alas, she was killed in a car crash; but he has since married again.

Charles and Dave were the professional singers; later, I also made a modest living at it, though this was more or less an accident. Peter, however, soon got a job at Dean Close School, and has been there ever since. He came from a rather remarkable sixth form at King Edward's, Birmingham; other members, also reading English, were the comedian Bill Oddie, and the late David Munrow, the early music man, who in those days was merely a bassoon player. Peter and I were thrown together; in our first year we shared a sitting-room, and we were always paired for supervisions. He was moody, amusing, slightly brittle. His father was an ironmonger, an entirely honourable trade, it seemed to me; but Peter had a chip about it. He regarded himself as more intelligent than I, and though pleased enough with his II ii in Part II, was slightly miffed when I got one, too. When we went down, he divided our books into two heaps, taking the ones he liked, and leaving me several duplicates.

There was plenty of music outside the chapel, of course. There were college concerts, arranged by undergraduates, at which we tried out our solo songs. There were May Week concerts. David invited Sir Arthur Bliss to one of these, to conduct his *Pastoral: Lie strewn the white flocks;* Sir Arthur seemed not to have heard of counter-tenors, and was puzzled when they did not join in with the tenors and basses. Another May Week we did the Brahms *Liebeslieder* Waltzes, which provoked a *bon mot* from Mike Boswell, the Yorkshire bass. "Ee," said Bos, "what that man Brahms can do with three-four time is nobody's business."

I remember doing Schutz in a small group with John Eliot Gardiner, who sang tenor in those days. John (I refused to call him 'Jiggy') tried to get into the King's choir as a volunteer (the choir contained two volunteers, as well as twelve choral scholars), but was pipped by Sebastian

Forbes. Later, I sang for him in London; he was good, but self-regarding and self-satisfied, and I never liked him.

Small groups flourished – the Aeolian Singers, the Ionian Consort. Noel Osborne's Aeolians once sacked their soprano overnight; we did an impromptu male voice programme instead. The poor girl was replaced by Margaret Cable, not an undergraduate, but living in Cambridge and studying at the Royal College. When she decided she was really a mezzo, she sent us Sarah Walker, later to have quite a distinguished career of her own, also as a mezzo. Sarah (Sally) was a lively lady in those days, though I never seemed to get my turn.

Noel was not a great organiser. We once had to do an almost instant Bach cantata concert, which went surprisingly well. He was a Jesus man, reading Classics, though for his last two years he read almost nothing at all. Many of us stopped going to lectures; Noel gave up supervisions as well. After he went down, he discovered that he could re-sit his degree in the following year, but not in the same subject; he taught himself History, and got a First, which rather startled his college. He became a hard-working and successful publisher; his Phillimore Press does local history, and has published a complete Doomsday Book.

It was Noel who, years later, attempted to deputise at three different cathedrals on the same day: Matins and Eucharist at Winchester, Evensong at Chichester, Advent Carols at Salisbury. Having set it all up, he had to pull out with a sore throat.

In my second year, the college paid for us to have singing lessons with John Carol Case. John had been an alto choral scholar, who soon switched to baritone; he had a rather limited voice, which he managed with great musicality over a long career. He taught me little about production, but was good on French song. I learnt more about production from Margaret Cable. "I can't stand this unsupported tone," she said briskly – and I discovered what support meant.

There were lots of solo opportunities. I did Fauré whenever possible, but also Schubert, Gurney, Warlock. Once I learnt some Webern, just to see if I could. I remember a Bach *Magnificat* at Royston, a *Messiah* at Histon, a *Creation* somewhere else.

All this time I was supposed to be reading English – but there were more important things in life. It was so good just to be there; for months I wandered around like a tourist. The freedom from rules and regulations was exhilarating; I could go to bed late, listen to opera all morning, watch cricket at Fenners. I discovered drinking, and getting drunk. I would like to say that I discovered girls, but I only really discovered one, and that not until my third year.

There were people to meet – the extraordinary Brian Burrows, for instance. Brian was a John's tenor, and a fantasist. The first time I met him, aged eighteen, he described singing at the Aldeburgh Festival with Peter Pears. Later, he was going to be installed as Lord of the Manor somewhere. When he became engaged, to a lady of quite eminent parentage, he invented (for the benefit of *The Times*) some distinguished parents of his own. His finances, too, were largely fantasy. He was convincing, and we were naïve; but every now and again, he told us something true. He once came to an Aeolian rehearsal with a programme which showed him as one of a group of prestigious soloists. There was something slightly wrong with the name; I think it was not him at all. But at the same time he told us that he knew the Controller of BBC Welsh Radio, and that he could get us a broadcast – which he did.

Or there was Richard Baker, and the spectacle provided by his succession of serious girl-friends. Richard was Keith's fellow alto; they had been choristers together. Unfortunately, the girl-friends tended to be more serious than Richard; there would be periods of tension, and it would all end in tears. Forty years later, Richard is still unmarried.

Then there was Philip Brett. Like Peter Cairns, his home circumstances were comparatively humble – I think he had a mother in Nottingham; but unlike Peter, he had no chip. He seemed gentle, and very English; he wore shabby sports coats and grey flannel trousers. He was a research student, doing Renaissance music; he edited our Taverner. I remember his being worried about a girl called Margaret, who was engaged to a fellow-student; he did not think they were right for each other. I wondered if he was keen on her himself. He went to America – and a year or two later he was back with long hair and beads, aggressively gay. I sometimes saw articles of his about gay issues in Britten operas, not all of which I agreed with. He was right about Margaret; the marriage broke up. "They even argued about *musica ficta*," someone told me.

And then there were adventures, such as the night we stole the Rubens. The big broadcast of the year was the Christmas Eve carol service, after which we went to The Eagle, had dinner in Hall, and returned to The Eagle till closing time. Then it was back to Chapel to sing the Tallis *Lamentations*; we let ourselves in with the organ scholar's key. This, I was told, was a tradition.

By my second year, the college had acquired the Rubens *Adoration of the Magi*, which was in its temporary position on a rostrum in the antechapel. Peter, who was not entirely sober, contrived to bump into this, and an alarm went off; but it did not seem to matter much, and we began on the Tallis. The police were round in no time; I still remember the sound of the sirens interrupting *Aleph*. I also remember standing in front of the Dean, Alec Vidler, at about one o'clock in the morning; he was wearing a woollen dressing gown. Michael Jaffé, Fellow and Rubens expert, thought that we ought have been sent down; in fact, we paid £5 to the Police Benevolent Fund.

Or there was the contest for the Lammas Shield. The latter was of Britannia-like proportions and made of papier-maché; it was a relic of some theatricals. The winner was to be he who collected the most of those red lamps which used to surround roadworks. The other competitors were Keith, and Sebastian Forbes (now Professor of Music at Surrey). After we had collected what seemed like rather a lot, we decided (it was Keith's idea) to arrange them in a neat line on top of Gibbs building. We felt that someone ought to admire this, so we called out Wilfred from the Porters' Lodge. "Very nice, sir," he said, and went back in. (He was a gem: "Let me shine my torch, to make it easier for you, sir," he would say, as one climbed in over Clare gate.) Keith won the shield; Sebastian was a poor third. Later, we smuggled it into Evensong and rolled it along the choir stalls.

Keith and Richard were not short of ideas. On the day of the Orlando Gibbons *obit* (June 6th), they decided that we would sing the *Short Service* morning canticles, Dec and Can, from either side of the Cam; this we did at about 8 a.m. Philip Radcliffe, the benign and elderly music don, told us how much he enjoyed it. Happening to be in Cambridge a few years later, I asked if it still went on. "Oh yes," I was told, "it's a tradition." A few years later still, no one knew anything about it.

I was fortunate, as a choral scholar, to enter Cambridge by one of the few remaining back doors. I had my two

'A' levels; Keith had one. The late Mike Hartley, who left without a degree, had a mere five 'O' levels, which was supposed to be the minimum requirement. A few years on, none of us would have been let near the place.

Perhaps I did a little more work than I remember. I do recall a period when Keith, Peter and I would make our way to the University Library in time for coffee; then there was lunch, and soon after three we left for evensong, imagining we had done a day's work. But I certainly wrote plenty of essays; one a week was the rule. I destroyed them all later. Somehow, I acquired a Third in Part One and a II ii in Part Two.

My first tutor was John Broadbent, one of the left-wing group of King's dons who disapproved of the chapel; he had just written a book on Milton. Later I had John Gross, who became editor of the *TLS*; fortunately, he talked a lot, which meant that I did not have to. Peter and I also went to a rather nice research student called Andrew Gurr, who is now an authority on Shakespeare's stage.

Sometimes we were farmed out. For one of my third year papers (for the life of me, I cannot remember its title) we would walk over to Churchill to see George Steiner. He was quite young then, a funny-looking little man whom my Uncle Graham once compared to Gollum in *The Lord of the Rings*. I knew that I knew nothing, and he seemed to know everything; he was keen on the King's choir, though, which helped. Supervisions were nominally from 2.30 to 3.30, but George insisted that we were 'adult', which meant that we stayed for as long as it took, and were offered port or sherry at four o'clock. This seemed to me an odd definition of 'adult' – and an odd choice of drinks for the time of day. Peter and I usually left early, to go to choir practice. I remember doing a long paper on the Jacobean court masque. This got off to a sticky start as I had apparently omitted a vital book from the bibliography;

but the actual paper went rather well. I reproduced much of it in my finals; hence (quite likely) my II ii.

He certainly knew a great deal, but not absolutely everything. Years later, I mentioned him to Edward Craig, my childhood friend, who is now a Cambridge Philosophy Professor and Fellow of Churchill. Edward told me that George was convincing on all manner of subjects – except one's own. "He says things which aren't true," said Edward. I think I had always suspected an element of bullshit.

What Cambridge English gave me was a framework. I picked up some enthusiasms, such as the poetry of Sir Thomas Wyatt; but I read far too little. I made up for it later, not only the obvious things, but swathes of stuff my tutors would hardly have thought of – the complete novels of Trollope, for instance. I am grateful for the framework, and for my tutors' forbearance; they must have found me very dull.

As I am grateful for much else. King's was a liberal college. It tolerated extremes without fuss, which has always seemed to me the mark of a civilised society. It did not bother too much about exeats, climbing in after midnight, or girls in people's rooms. It encouraged informal relations between dons and undergraduates – as did other colleges; but King's had done so since the nineteenth century. The Chetwynd Society, a sort of undergraduate prank and drinking club, had the Lay Dean as an *ex officio* member; the Lay Dean was in charge of student discipline.

I shall add a few random highlights. Old E.M.Forster pottering across the front court on the way to his rooms, in a shabby flat cap and an awful mac. (I never dared to speak to him.) Peter Pears and Julian Bream doing lute songs in the Music School on my twentieth birthday (and port in my room afterwards). Pears and Britten's *Winterreise* in the Town Hall; I can still remember the way Britten linked two sections of *Fruhlingstraum*. The night of the Cuban missile crisis, when I sat on the floor of Peter's room with (of all things) a bottle of Benedictine, half convinced (all of us) that the world was going to end. The Chetwynd Society leading the cattle from the college field round the front court, and receiving a (fake) letter from the Provost asking them to clear up the mess. A *Gerontius* in Chapel which almost knocked me out of my atheism...

But I have left the best till last. The story of how I met Janet is complicated. Her younger sister, Anne, was in her third year at Girton when I went up, and became engaged to Roy Bean, who was a bass volunteer. Janet would visit Anne in Cambridge, and I saw her for the first time on the croquet lawn in the Fellows' Garden (she does not remember this); I wondered which sister was the elder.

In the Long Vacation I joined a small tenor-and-bass group, the Baccholian Singers, whose aim was to holiday in Cornwall, sleeping in a barn and singing round pubs and clubs to raise money for spastics. Janet and Anne's parents lived in Plymouth, so in my second year it was decided (not by me) to break our journey and do two nights there. I slept in the Steers' front room, not sleeping much, as it happened, as their mantelpiece clock chimed every fifteen minutes. Apparently my future mother-in-law was impressed by my willingness to dry dishes.

I remember Janet being fairly scornful about our rehearsal; she was never a choir groupie. It emerged that she had a new teaching job in Cambridge, starting in September. Out of mere politeness, I suggested that she come to see me – and thought no more about it.

She had been learning to drive, and in late September passed her test. Knowing no one in Cambridge, but wanting to tell somebody, she found me. After that we saw more of each other. She would come to Chapel and sketch the fan-vaulting. (I still have this on a Christmas card.) We talked a lot. We thought we were just good friends.

In the New Year she came to Liverpool to stay with her pal Isobel Ross, and I suggested that they take the train out to Formby. It was snowing. Janet played the piano for me. An Ormskirk farmer always gave Father a goose at New Year – so we ate Joe Cropper's goose. Father claimed afterwards not to remember which girl was which.

Janet and I made our separate ways back to Cambridge – and anyone can imagine the rest. I remember meals (steak and asparagus) cooked on a gas-ring in my gyp room... Other meals in Janet's flat in St Barnabas Road (she kept half bottles of Nuits St George under the book-case)... A walk in the Fellows' Garden in the snow... A May Ball... Both our mothers dashing up to Cambridge in succession to see what was going on (mine pretended she was visiting her sister)... All four parents to tea in my room, and the Fellows' Garden again...

We were married on September 11th, barely a year after the driving test. Cambridge had been wonderful, irresponsible. Real life was about to begin.

Four

SCHOOLS

I HAD never intended to be a teacher. At one time I had hoped to be a professional singer, but this would have required further training, and I was not really sure that I had the talent. Besides, by February, 1963, I was engaged to be married, and was clearly expected to keep Janet in the style to which she was accustomed. So rather late in the day I began applying to boys' preparatory schools, through Gabbitas and Thring; in due course, I was appointed to Seafield School, in Little Common, near Bexhill-on-Sea.

Bexhill was full of old people, but it also contained a number of small private schools, most of which have now closed down. To start with, we lived in one room; the school had promised a house, but this took time. We were newlyweds, so it did not seem to matter. It was in our one room that I had mumps.

Seafield itself was a family school, founded in 1904; by 1963 it was in the hands of a father and son. It lived in a time-warp; when there was talk of an inspection, a colleague wondered why we needed another, since nothing had changed since the beginning. The father, Granville Coghlan, was a nice old boy who, in his old-fashioned way, knew what he was doing; he had been a Cambridge rugby blue. Manners were important, and so was Latin; when the end-of-term marks were added up, there was a maximum of 400 for Latin, but only 100 for English. This to him was quite logical. There were no staff meetings and no parents' meetings. But he had the boys' interests at heart.

The son, however, was somewhat different; he was a jumped-up twit, whose priorities were to look important and to be popular. On the school notepaper, he was 'T.Dip. IAPS', which was the teaching qualification of the Incorporated Association of Preparatory Schools. It looked good, and was longer than his father's 'M.A., Cantab.', but a colleague, similarly qualified, told me it was not worth the paper it was written on. Years later, I met somebody who had come across him; after the school closed down he (allegedly) bought an office stationery business, went broke, left his wife and children, eloped with a Battle Abbey sixth-former, and was last heard of as a milkman.

There was a third headmaster. J.A.C.Kempston ('Jack') was well into his seventies, and moved on tramlines. His teaching consisted largely of dictated notes which had to be learnt. I was assured by David Swann that he had been made a head after forty years' service because this was cheaper that giving him a clock. (They were notoriously mean. David and I, after an hour's bowling in the nets, were once offered a glass of sherry by old Granville. It turned out to be just that: one small glass, which we shared. Granville also did nothing about my pension; it saved him the contributions.)

Three headmasters, and a certain lack of communication, sometimes led to problems. We once decided that the school motto ought to be *Alii alia dicunt*: 'some say one thing, some another'.

David Swann was the only other young man on the staff; he soon left. The best of them was John Lewis, an energetic Welshman who taught Latin, and was quite a good musician. Others had mainly retired from something else: Charles Howe, a retired colonial administrator, Bill Tyrell, a retired Lieutenant-Colonel, Freddie Quinn-Young, a retired policeman who had seen service in both Rhodesia and Hong Kong. There was a groundsman, Bill Simms, who introduced me to Little Common cricket club, and his assistant, the Mohican. There was also a *Carry On*-films busty matron.

My hours were extraordinary. Because it was a boarding school, I had to be there for breakfast at a quarter to eight; I left after supper, about twelve hours later. I had one half day a week, and was on duty for one Sunday in three. On the 'off' Sundays, I was free after church, at mid-day; duty Sundays were another twelve-hour stint, with an hour off at tea-time. (It was in one of these hours off, we think, that Jonathan was conceived.)

As to my teaching, much of it was not very good. I had drifted into education with little thought, and no one helped me. I had a degree, and was supposed to be an expert. There was no syllabus. There were hardly any books; my predecessor had taught mainly grammar, out of his head. I tried to get some creative writing going; early on, we won prizes in a local poetry competition, which pleased old Granville, and later I started a small magazine. I also taught a little French, deducing what I ought to teach from the books I had been given (just as I partly deduced the English syllabus from Public School Common Entrance papers). I had nothing to do with the music; John Lewis took the choir, and the rest was done by a little Welsh lady called Miss Phillips. She and John spoke Welsh together. When Jonathan arrived (rather unexpectedly in the middle of the night), she told me that it was lucky to be born into the snow.

There was also sport. I was expected to coach rugby, which I hated, football, which I quite liked but was out of touch with, and of course cricket. Granville had a bad leg, so I helped him with the First XI. In my third year we had rather a poor side. After several disasters, Granville decided to spend a whole session on the forward and back defensive strokes. "If you learn these two," I found myself saying, "there's no reason why you shouldn't stay in all afternoon." It was true. One little lad, who had never been anything but a cross-batter before, suddenly started to look immaculate. We sent him in first – and he batted right through the innings for 13 not out. He never did it again; he got bored with himself. But it was a masterly piece of coaching.

I was at Seafield for three years. In the end it was my parents who suggested that I ought to have a proper teaching qualification. They were right. So I enrolled at the Cambridge University Department of Education, and went back to being a student.

We lived – Janet, Jonathan and I – in a seventeenth-century cottage in Harston, about six miles out of Cambridge. It belonged to the Lord Lieutenant of the county, who inhabited the adjacent grand house. Firewood was free, and his wife would appear from time to time with baskets of produce. There was no proper sanitation, so the rent was remarkably low.

The best of my education year was the teaching practice, and tutorials with Raymond O'Malley. Raymond O'Malley had taught for many years at Dartington, the sort of progressive school where lessons were voluntary. In spite of this, he was sensible, intelligent and benign. I remember him saying, just before the exams, that if any of us failed he would eat his hat in the market-place. He was, I realised afterwards, perfectly safe. One gentleman had retired early when it emerged that he had only stayed on to play rugby;

another failed to survive teaching practice. But at this time, and for some years afterwards, there were more jobs than teachers, and almost everybody passed.

My teaching practice was at The Friends' School, Saffron Walden – mixed, secondary and Quaker. It was a good place, largely because of the Quaker ethos. There was a school council, staff and pupils, with real decision-making powers. Though an old school, it had no obvious traditions; everything was up for discussion. They had without fuss abolished their prefect system not long before I arrived, on the grounds that the duties could be shared out among sixth-formers. And everyone was of equal value. The staff list contained not only teaching, but also cooking, cleaning and gardening staff. The school magazine did not distinguish between staff and student editors. Occasionally there seemed to be too lengthy discussions of rather trivial points; but the principle was good.

I took little part in university life, though Janet and I both joined the Madrigal Society. Raymond Leppard conducted, queening around in a velvet jacket. I remember some Monteverdi, and Samuel Barber's *Reincarnations*, as well as the standard English madrigalists; but the society was in decline, and abolished itself soon after we left. For the rest, we had a one-year-old child and a life of our own. My parents were living in Great Bardfield, only fifty minutes away, and we saw a lot of them. Mother came to baby-sit on madrigal nights.

By June, 1967, therefore, I was a qualified teacher, and had begun looking for jobs in Prep Schools again. This, I think, was a safety-first move; I returned to what I knew. Soon enough, I was appointed Head of English at Homefield School, Sutton, Surrey. It was not very difficult. The headmaster, Martin Carnes, had also been a King's choral scholar, which in his mind removed the need for formalities such as interviews. He simply assumed that he was going to offer me the job, and that I would accept it. So we bought our house in Norman Road, Sutton, where Tristram was born, and where we have lived ever since. When the school moved to a new building on its old playing field, it was just over our fence.

Martin Carnes was not a good headmaster. He would walk around with a pained expression on his face, as though something was just about to go wrong, which it often was. He would lose his temper at inappropriate moments – a staff leaving party, for instance. And he had no sense of priorities: lost property was the bane of his life, and took an inordinate amount of time.

My colleagues, by and large, were a better bunch than those at Seafield. Old Patrick Doyley was clearly past it; if he could not remember a boy's face, he wrote on his report, 'Has yet to make his mark'. But he soon left, and was replaced by Laurie Jones, a forty-five-year-old keen schoolboy. David Evans was the sort of elderly bachelor who lived with his father; he taught Latin, and was clearly very competent. George Stafford was of the old, unqualified school; he taught Maths, rather boringly. Darcy Colley *was* qualified, he told us: "I have letters after my name." These turned out to be FRGS – Fellow of the Royal Geographical Society; one acquires them by paying a small fee. The boys used to present him with knotty problems in order to hear him say (yet again), "I require notice of that question." Towards the end of my time he began looking for jobs elsewhere, and was understandably miffed to receive from an agency a description of his own job. The headmaster wanted to replace him – but had not got round to telling him.

There were two young men, Tony Packwood and Trevor Worton. Tony (PE and Maths) was amiable, a little idle, and not very bright; he never moved on, and I was recently asked to his retirement party. Trevor came from an army family, and was greatly disappointed when the army turned him down. During my third year the head asked Trevor to add Geography to his History teaching; Trevor declined, on the grounds that he did not know any. The result was that he was sacked. This caused great unhappiness. There were indignation meetings. The head claimed it was the governors' decision, while they said it was the head's; Martin walked around looking more pained than ever, and relationships became rather strained. It was my first experience of the sort of situation which can take more time and nervous energy than the job itself.

Trevor was replaced by David Child-Thomas. David, a few years younger than I, had left school with one 'O' level, and had pulled himself up by his own bootstraps via night school and the College of Preceptors. He was full of ideas about education, and soon realised that he had made a mistake in coming to Homefield. He gave in his notice after three weeks, which must have been rather startling to poor Martin Carnes; he moved on to Bedales. By this time I, too, was in need of a change. David and I taught for only a year together, but we have been friends ever since.

I felt that I had achieved quite a lot at Homefield, far more than I had at Seafield. I was young and enthusiastic, and was no longer making it up as I went along. Martin Carnes had bought a new course book for the whole school just before I arrived, without consulting me; it was hopeless, and I hardly used it. I got a lot of reading going, and discussion about reading. I took over the school magazine, and introduced a creative writing section. I was keen on the creative writing side, particularly poetry, and we began winning prizes in local and national competitions. The *Daily Mirror* ran an annual children's poetry competition in those days, in which we had several successes; we also won another competition which involved a trip to Yorkshire to collect a prize from John Betjeman. The winner was Michael Bracewell, an amusing child who later became a novelist.

I did some improvised drama (a legacy of my education year – Martin Carnes did not approve of it), and began putting on plays. I started with a one-acter, and moved on to a shortened *Henry V*; I had no stage experience, and learnt as I went. None of the cast was older than thirteen. In my final year we did a cut-down *Tempest*; it is a play which I revere, and I still remember the awe with which I chose Ferdinand's logs in Nonesuch Park. I wrote my own music, including songs for Ariel. The part was played by a curious child who eighteen months previously had gone off the rails and become rather peculiar. By now, he was right back on form; I gave him the songs on a Friday night, and by Monday he knew them by heart. Rehearsals were a joy. I would emphasise to the boys the difference between professionals and amateurs. This had nothing to do with ability. Professionals learnt their parts by the deadline, came to rehearsals on time, helped out other actors and cleared up afterwards. There were no amateurs. Costumes, props, scenery were much more elaborate than for *Henry V*. Two parents spent ages constructing a lighting system. And then – 'Our revels now are ended'. After I left, my poor successor was lumbered with Shakespeare for years; Martin Carnes told him it was a tradition.

I started a choir, because there did not seem to be one. I remember doing some of Britten's *Friday Afternoon* songs, including the four-part canon, 'Old Abram Brown'. I also wrote a small opera for them, called *The Lotos Eaters*, based on *The Odyssey*, and a carol, *There is no rose*, bits of which I recycled later.

Then there was sport. I was allocated to the Under Elevens, cricket and football. I briefly became very keen on football coaching, to the point of attending an FA coaching course in the evenings. After a poor first year, we got to work. Our most difficult opponents were Dulwich College Prep; they had four times as many boys as we did, and a pernickety and Teutonic coach who wore real referee's black clothes. In my second year we played them early on, and lost 8-0. By the return, we were much improved, and they were blasé. We scored the only goal of the game ten minutes into the second half, and hung on grimly for the final half hour. In the following year, we were unbeaten.

Funny things happen in Under Eleven cricket. I remember a wonderful moment when the two batsmen and the ball arrived at the same end simultaneously; the bails were removed, and I said, "Not out". There was a pause; everyone knew that somebody ought to be out somehow. Then the penny dropped, and there was a chase for the other end. After Trevor left, I ran the First XI; I encouraged a lot of spin bowling.

I stayed at Homefield for four years. My next school was Ravensbourne School for Boys, Bromley. Again, the job was not hard to come by; I was the only applicant. This was partly because I delivered my application by hand during a postal strike, but also because of the supply and demand situation; if anyone half-way decent turned up, I was told, they were almost certain to be appointed.

Ravensbourne was something of a shock. It was not a good school, and in some ways was rather corrupt. It was a comprehensive, formed by the recent amalgamation of Bromley Boys Grammar School and the Secondary Modern across the road. Grammar School teachers spoke openly about having to join the riff-raff, and the Secondary Modern staff also thought that they had been better off as they were. The Secondary Modern head was still in his old buildings, but only in charge of the First Year; the Grammar head, who was running the whole show, sat in his office and pretended it was still a Grammar School. The Deputy Head was having a breakdown on the job. Discipline was not good, and any holding operation had to come from the middle; it was certainly not coming from the top. As to corruption, a good example was the free lunch list. If you ran a lunchtime activity, you got a free lunch; if you stopped the activity, you stayed on the list and went on eating the lunch. The Deputy Head and his two cronies were timetabled to have Friday afternoons off; they sat in his office, played cards and drank gin. I naively assumed that playground duty was done in the playground; the Ravensbourne method was to play snooker in the staff-room, and look out of the window every ten minutes.

I learnt to work the system. Discovering from my Head of Department which forms I was due to be teaching, I picked out a particularly amiable bunch and approached the timetabler (a flunkey in the Technical Drawing department). "John," I asked, "may I be form master of 2B next year?" "I'm not in charge of these things," he replied, "but I'll pencil it in if you like." No one ever altered his pencil markings, and I had a trouble-free year.

But it was all rather different to what I was used to. My only secondary teaching had been at the polite Friends' School; some of those I was now teaching were not polite at all. So I learnt survival. Then there was sixth form teaching; in my first year I did Chaucer's *Troilus and Criseyde*, *The Waste Land* and *1984*. This required serious preparation; some (not all) of my pupils were rather bright. I took to preparing sixth form work on summer holidays; my Chaucers usually had sand in them.

I became a qualified football referee; the Head of P.E., who needed plenty of people to take his games, used to run courses for staff and sixth-formers. One could become qualified at the lowest level merely by sitting an exam. I now had a black shirt of my own; years later, I gave it to a tramp outside Victoria Station. But I was not a good referee: it all went by too fast. Umpiring was easier. I ran the second-year cricket team, driving them to away matches in the school mini-bus. (If your vehicle is large enough, I discovered, people get out of your way.) The games were on Saturday mornings. I was playing myself for Sutton at the time, so after leaving Bromley at about 1.15, I would drive rather fast to wherever my own fixture was, eating a sandwich as I went. Ten or fifteen years later, this sort of voluntary activity had almost disappeared.

I got involved in more drama – *The Tempest* again, in which I assisted a young man called Dave Ashbee. He was not very organised, and I was not too pleased with the results. But I discovered the Dramatic Society, a collection of boy stage-hands who spent their lunch hours under the stage like troglodytes, waiting for a play to turn up. I also discovered how to placate the caretaker. It left me better prepared for the next venture.

This was rather delightful. Some sixth-formers decided that they wanted to put on *The Importance of Being Ernest*; having cast it, and made various arrangements, they asked me to produce. I had to put up with a pantomime-dame Lady Bracknell, but in fact the cast was rather good; we borrowed a Gwendolyn and Cecily from Ravensbourne School for Girls. Because the boys felt it was their show, I was saved a lot of trouble which might otherwise have fallen to my lot. They invited the Head of Art to design the sets, someone else to do front of house. They designed posters; they hired costumes from French's; they provided me with a runner. I loved the rehearsals; certain lines made me laugh not once but almost every time. I was surprised, too, to discover how Algernon's love scene with Cecily, so one-dimensional on the page, becomes at least two-dimensional with real actors.

This was my last production. They completely take over your life, and need a lot of energy. In my final year at Ravensbourne I was mildly unwell, and did not feel up to it. At my next school there was a real expert in place, so I left it to him.

I had some slightly rough times at Ravensbourne, but also some good ones. My head of department, Leonard Taylor, took to me for some reason, and was very kind; we spent our lunch hours preparing boys for the Poetry Society's verse speaking exams. It was at Ravensbourne, too, that I first taught Harold Brighouse's Lancashire play, *Hobson's Choice*. As a Lancastrian myself, I quickly devised four simple rules for speaking Lancashire; some of the boys became rather good at it – particularly the one who spoke only Italian at home.

I left Ravensbourne almost on a whim. Leonard Taylor, who was ageing and had nervous problems, was looking for something easier. Flipping through his *Times Ed.*, I found a job at Hinchley Wood School, Esher, whose Head of English, Peter Dale, I already knew. Everything had to be tied up by May 31st, and it was already the middle of the month, but I applied to see what would happen. I was not quite the only applicant, but the other one, I discovered, was an internal candidate who had already blotted her copybook, so the thing fell into my lap.

Hinchley Wood when I went there was a going concern. It had begun as a mixed secondary modern, but because the percentage of grammar school places in the area was particularly low, some fairly bright children came our way. The previous head, rather against the wish of the local authority, had added a sixth form. The school's strength was in helping lame dogs over stiles; children of fairly modest ability, if they were prepared to work, found themselves passing more exams than they might have expected. Compared with Ravensbourne, I found it unpretentious, efficient and welcoming.

The headmaster, Mr. Davies, was the only good head I worked for. 'Devious Davies', some called him; he could fix anything. If, for instance, you found yourself with three weeks' jury service in Kingston during the run-up to 'A' levels, "Leave it with me," he would say; "I know the man who arranges it." 'Leave it with me' was a favourite phrase; sometimes it was a way of keeping you happy without his having to do anything at all. He was also good at fixing the school boilers. He was very quiet. Once, he came into my classroom so silently that I did not know he was there. I was in full flow; he was too polite to interrupt.

His deputy, Miss Mount, was a formidable lady; a colleague said that she always made him feel he had a fly button undone. She would leave you in what felt like mid-conversation; to her, everything had been said. She was very good at her job. Meeting her years later in Chichester, I found I had put an arm round her; I was glad to see her. Had I done so at Hinchley Wood, it would have sent shock waves through the building.

The second deputy, Mr. Macfarlan, was less formidable, but a calming influence. When he retired, Miss Mount read excerpts from an inspectors' report of 1946. The buildings were run down, the staff inadequate, and morale was low; but young Mac's woodwork department shone like a beacon. They were a good team.

The school's virtues were solid and old-fashioned – in some ways very old-fashioned indeed. Boys did metalwork, woodwork and mechanical drawing; girls did needlework and cookery. (Very thick girls did typing.) I remember Miss Mount defending this policy: "We let a girl do mechanical drawing once, but it didn't work; she gave it up after two terms." I hardly dared to point out that one was not a fair statistical sample. Discipline, too, was rigid. I was more or less used to classes being quiet when I entered the room, but the first class I took looked as though it had been sitting in silence for at least ten minutes. The downside was that, to start with, one could hardly get some of them to talk at all. They were not used to talking; they were used to being told things.

I was appointed as second in the English department, to do a large share of sixth form work; Peter Dale was overburdened. Within a few days, I was also asked to run the library; I had no experience, but it paid more, so I agreed. This was in the days when the librarian taught a full time-table, and fitted the library into odd moments. When time caught up with us ten or twelve years later, I was replaced by a full-time librarian with a part-time assistant.

There were, I think, seven in the English department when I started; later we grew smaller. The constants during my time (1974-1990) were Peter Dale and Lionel Barnes. Lionel, about ten years older than I, had been made redundant by Shell and had just retrained as a teacher; he was an old fuss-pot, but I liked him. He reminded me of the White Rabbit. Peter, even at that stage, was already quite a distinguished poet and translator. As Head of Department, he was both imaginative and practical. He was also opinionated, and had a fairly short fuse. I soon learned that his bark was worse than his bite, and that if one barked back he climbed down. Others did not learn this; two polite ladies would sometimes appeal to me to speak to him on their behalf after he had snapped at them. There was no malice in it; he was a kind man underneath. Towards the end of my time, when I was becoming more and more frustrated and difficult, he was particularly patient. I mentioned this in my leaving speech, to the mild surprise of some of my colleagues, who could not imagine a patient Peter; but it was true. He was a keen cyclist; once, when my car broke down, we rather startled the children by arriving on a tandem.

I enjoyed those early years; the sixth-form teaching was stimulating, and the place was well-run. A very competent lady dealt with the remedial work, and another member of the department also specialised in lower ability forms, so I had little to do with the blunt end. I also preferred the mixed environment, so much more natural for teaching literature; in an all-boys' school, the attitudes are akin to those of a rugby club bar.

It did not last. Over several years there were changes within the school, and in education as a whole. As far as the school went, we lost, over a fairly short period, both our sixth form and (through retirement) the whole top management team. I missed the sixth form, and for a while applied for other jobs, but perhaps I was a little half-hearted; the other half still liked the school, and waited to see how it would turn out. After a few years, it seemed too late to move. I was not a good career builder.

The new management team was rather different. The head, Gerry Parker, had a loud voice and a fairly small brain. He initiated almost nothing; he merely reacted to things, too quickly and with little thought. His latest scheme was always followed by a trail of people into his office saying, "But, Headmaster..." The trick was to go in last; he usually agreed with the last person who spoke to him. His main virtue was openness; one did know exactly what was going on. He was a little wary of Peter and me, since as published poets we were, he thought, probably more intelligent than he was. But he was good about subsidising my school poetry magazine.

The two deputies were contrasted. One was an oleaginous toad, whom it makes me cross to think about. The other, Frances Thornton, was something new to Hinchley

Wood: an educational theorist. She had a rather hard time with the Hinchley Wood traditionalists, but she kept at it. She had a pigeon-holing mind; concepts that had floated rather hazily round one's brain would be pinned down in neat phrases. I remember her seminars on discipline. Several of my colleagues were waiting for the bit where we decided how actually to *punish* children; she was more interested in what had gone wrong in the first place. (A simple example: confusion about where a crowd of yobs were to take an exam produced a near riot in the corridor. Of course they ought not to have rioted – but the situation could easily have been avoided.) This was not only sensible, it was also practical; by this time there were almost no ways in which one was allowed to punish children anyway. Because of library duties, I often had a late lunch with her and another divorced lady; I enjoyed the verbal sparring about education, in which she briefly revived my interest. I also learnt a lot about divorce. "The world is made for couples," they both told me; the single room supplement is merely one example.

As to education itself, Hinchley Wood, like Seafield, had been in a time-warp from which we were rudely jolted by an inspection. We still had a good reputation, but we were not a good school; we were coasting. From 1981 to 1984, I was a lay clerk at Guildford Cathedral, singing eight services a week on top of full time teaching; a few years later, this would not have been possible.

But it was not just the inspection; the times were changing. When I began teaching, there was little accountability; it was assumed that one knew what one was doing, and one was left to get on with it. This was fine if things were working; if they were not, chaos ruled unchecked, often for years. I remember a middle-aged colleague at Ravensbourne. One would glance through his glass door and see him holding forth with a book in his hand; his class in the meantime would be chatting, playing cards, wandering about the room or creating various sorts of mayhem. All parties seemed quite happy with this arrangement. Of course it was utterly wrong. But now the pendulum seemed to have swung the other way, and one had to be accountable for absolutely everything. This involved endless department meetings, faculty meetings, year teachers' meetings, minutes, redrafting of syllabuses, schemes of work, mission statements… It was all very worthy, but it took a huge amount of time, which was largely wasted as no one read much of what was written, or took any notice of it if they did. On more that one occasion, Peter, Lionel and I had a quick chat in break, after which we all went home early and Peter invented the minutes.

Government, too, suddenly would not leave education alone. GCSE replaced the old exam system. It was by no means a bad thing, but whereas the old 'O' level literature syllabus consisted of little more than a list of set books, to which one added some past papers, the new syllabus had pages and pages of stuff. Every other year there was a new initiative of some sort. The National Curriculum was raising its head about the time I left, but there were others: Records of Achievement, for instance, and something to do with technology which I never understood. In order to implement these initiatives you had to think like the people who invented them. As there was no overall plan, they did not necessarily relate to each other, but continued side by side, so that you had to have several ways of thinking to hand, apart from the way in which you naturally thought anyway. Frances Thornton told me that knowledge was power, and that one ought, therefore, to read all the documents that came one's way. I was not very interested in power, but I knew that these initiatives always got simpler as the moment for implementing them approached, so I saved myself a lot of time by reading nothing at all until the last possible moment.

Kenneth Baker, who was briefly Tory Education Minister, added to the control-freakery by imposing a new contract which, among other things, laid down minimum hours. One result of this was that any remaining goodwill towards voluntary activity disappeared for ever. Schools lost what I had always thought of as the unofficial curriculum. When I went to Hinchley Wood, school plays were in the care of the Head of History, John Hancock, who himself lived in a sort of cinematic fantasy world. He teamed up with the new Head of Music, John Sutton, to put on a series of rather good musicals: *The Boy Friend, West Side Story*. Later we had a lady in the English department, an ineffectual teacher but very keen on horses; she would take teams of riders to compete against posh schools like Whitgift – and win. Now all of this disappeared; there was no longer the time.

One was suddenly required to learn new tricks – Pastoral Care, for instance. I argued, successfully, that 'pastoral' comes from *pastor*, a shepherd, and that true pastoral care consists of what we had always been doing: keeping a gentle eye on things, and intervening where necessary. So it was re-named; but it still involved playing silly games in form periods, and teaching things like health education, about which I knew nothing. Of course one could mug it up the night before, but I clung obstinately to the belief that one taught best what one had a broad knowledge of, and felt in one's bones.

All this was part of an assumption that you could turn teachers into clones. The English part of our inspection went quite well, but we were a little startled when it was suggested that we teach Caribbean literature; we lacked ethnic breadth. This might have made sense for people who believed in it, but Peter and I were a couple of old-style Oxbridge English graduates, and the chances of our doing it successfully were more or less nil. Sense talked about education, I once read, decreases as the square of the distance from the classroom.

Of course there were still things that I was enjoying. From time to time one is lucky enough to have a class which is not only bright and interested, but also works well together. I had to abandon one of these when I left; I had had another for the start of GCSE. As well as set books, the children now had to do Wider Reading, in poetry, prose and drama, and produce coursework on it. I raided the library, and filled my room with possibilities. Choosing their own tasks, they did work on Browning's dramatic monologues, Jane Austen's novels, a comparison between *Oedipus Rex* and Ibsen's *Ghosts*. They wrote sonnets for Orlando to pin to the trees in Arden; they turned bits of Hardy novels into ballads – and so on. By this time, we were receiving the whole ability range, including the top.

I also enjoyed being form master of one of the new-intake forms, a job I had done almost from the start. I would uncle them along for a term or so, and then watch them find their feet. I appreciated some of the more eccentric and non-aligned characters whom others found awkward. I remember trying to fill up my form's sports day programme; since we got one point merely for entering, it paid to have someone in each event. All sorts of cripples and fatties volunteered – but there was still the girls' 440. "What about it, Katie?" I said. "I *hate* running," she replied. The PE department thought I should have got heavy at this point, but I could only burst out laughing. I also taught the only girl at Hinchley Wood to get pregnant. She was supposed to be difficult, but she gave me no trouble. She got an 'A' in English Language – and failed everything else.

Then there was the poetry magazine; it was called *The Rowan Tree*, since there was one at the school gate. The first issue was typed by the school secretary, with a little artwork on the front and back cover. Then we became more ambitious. I teamed up with one of the art teachers, Sara Adams. Sara was about four feet eleven and totally involved in what she was doing. She and the other art teacher, Judy Searle, had transformed the school; any blank space in hall or corridors was filled with children's work. It was not only the bright children, either; all sorts of duffers and layabouts were producing good stuff. Poetry and art fed off each other. One of the best sets of poems I ever had emerged from the Butterfly Project; Sara had done so much work on butterflies that the poems came of their own accord. Other art was produced to go with pre-existing poems. One rule we had was that there were to be no formal meetings; everything was done through brief chats in corridors. It was quicker that way.

So now we had a poetry magazine with a lot of artwork. It grew. I initiated a competition for writing a Christmas carol – words first; then we sent the winning entry to the Music Department, who had their own competition to find a tune. The composers (one of whom was also the poet) performed it at the Christmas concert. I published words and music in *The Rowan Tree*.

The Business Studies Department became involved. The children word-processed the poems in the computer room, took over the marketing and attracted sponsors. We also diversified into Christmas cards, with verse and artwork by the pupils. We made a useful profit.

I cannot say that I planned all this; it evolved. But inspectors like inter-disciplinary activity, and briefly I found that I was a Very Modern Teacher. The magazine lasted one issue after I left, and then died. So did the tree.

All this buzz was invigorating – but there was still too

much pulling in the opposite direction. Disciplinary standards had slipped, as was almost inevitable; respect for any sort of authority – the police, the monarchy – had declined considerably over the years, and it could only be reflected in schools.

Our remedial teacher had left, and was not replaced; one had to do more and more of this sort of work oneself. I plugged away at it, but it was not really my scene.

And more and more I found I was running against contradictions which there was no resolving. We were compelled by law, for instance, to have a daily act of Christian worship – to behave, in fact, as though we were a Christian community; but ninety per cent of the staff were not Christian at all. And how does one persuade the least intelligent children that they are not the bottom of the heap and that there is still something in it for them? One cannot, and they take their disaffection out on the system.

One needs patience to teach; I was becoming increasingly impatient. I was fed up with being fed up all the time. "Sometimes," a colleague said to me, "I think it would be peaceful just to stack shelves in Sainsbury's." It sounded back-breaking to me, but I knew what she meant. I started looking around; anything would do. I was quite prepared to be bored; it would make a change from being hassled. I have described elsewhere how I found my new career. I had done twenty-seven years; it was enough.

Five

CRICKET

LIKE MANY small boys, I wanted to bowl as fast as I could. I practised in the holiday, and tried it out at school; I was ten. It was not a great success. I struck my knee with my bowling hand – something I have occasionally seen done in Test Matches; the ball trickles away in a random direction. Later in the over there was another disaster; perhaps I ran into the stumps. I was not asked to bowl again for a while – by which time I had discovered leg-breaks.

To begin with I bowled them from behind my ear, almost off the wrong foot; later, I read Clarrie Grimmett's book and made some adjustments. My front foot always came too wide, which made googlies difficult (though Robin Hobbs managed); I could bowl one off ten yards with a tennis ball, but never attempted it in the middle. This, of course, was later; to start with, I just did what came naturally. No one told me what to do. It seemed to me that if I were to hit the middle stump, I needed to pitch outside leg; this confused rather small boys, but was not a good idea in the long term. As to length, provided the ball did not bounce twice, one was probably along the right lines. I also thought I was a batsman, but it was such a small school that anyone was a batsman who was not a duffer. I took a few wickets for the first team, and scored a few runs.

At Uppingham, with First Eleven Colours on my CV, I was placed on a lofty school game. It was under the care of Mr. Lumsden, who umpired inscrutably from behind his moustaches, and left the running of it to the boys. The two captains made sure that they and their friends did all the batting and bowling, so I only fielded, and it was a relief to be relegated to the Leagues.

The Leagues (there were over and under sixteen versions) were rather jolly inter-house competitions for those not on an official school game. No one had heard of slow bowling in the Leagues, and it probably would not have been a good idea; boundaries were short, and fielding and wicket-keeping rough and ready. I became a slightly dour opening batsman, and bowled ineffective medium pace.

But in the holidays I returned to leg-breaks. Edward Craig's father was a keen cricketer. He was lame, and in club cricket had been a wicket-keeper batsman with a runner. He built a concrete net in their back garden, in which Edward and I practised endlessly. It soon became clear that we were poles apart. At fifteen, he was in the Charterhouse First Eleven; by the time he left, he had beaten all Peter May's school batting records. His great thing was concentration; he was a sort of Boycott, though without the selfishness. He would concentrate in the most casual net. I would hit his stumps about once a summer, always with a faster ball which pitched middle and leg and took the off bail. I wish I knew how I did this; I could have been a world-beater. I sometimes opened the batting with him for Formby schoolboys. One day, I remember, I thought I was doing quite well; after about twenty minutes, I had scored 9, and Edward 11. The next time I looked, I was still on nine, and Edward had passed fifty. We also did a lot of bowling; he bowled non-turning off-breaks.

I played little cricket in Cambridge – there were choir practices to go to. But there was an annual match against St. John's choral scholars, which we always won (it annoyed George Guest, their choirmaster). In my last year I took five wickets and carried my bat, in front of my admiring mother and my admiring fiancée. Father umpired, and Stuart, playing for us, held a magnificent catch wearing sailing kit and pince-nez sunglasses.

Edward, of course, played for Cambridge. I remember his first match. "You practise at Fenner's for three weeks," he told me; "then one day you are there again – but this time it's against Bedser and Lock." He made 10, with great determination; it was better than most of the others. Later, he scored several centuries, some of which I watched. He was neck and neck with Mike Brearley; they were the same age. They both scored 1,000 runs in the season, and played for the Gentlemen against the Players. In the vacation, he played a few games for Lancashire – not unsuccessfully, but it was the beginning of the end. He found the life, and the people, boring. He played two more years for Cambridge, with decreasing interest; in his fourth year, I think he played golf. He achieved a double first (better than Brearley), and soon became a Fellow of Churchill, where he has been ever since.

There remains his first University match. He was having a fling with my cousin Liz at the time; Liz was a flighty young lady who used to stay with us in the school holidays. After scoring a duck in the first innings, he was joined by Liz at the team's hotel – and scored a second innings hundred. I have always put that hundred down to Liz.

When I left Cambridge, I played for Little Common, near Bexhill. They were a village side, using a council ground, but the wickets were good because the groundsman was a member. I scored a few runs in my first year, and twice took some wickets. The following year they decided I was a batsman; I hardly bowled at all, until one day I was allowed a couple of overs before tea. I took a wicket in the first, and a hat-trick in the second. After that, I bowled a little more.

In my final year I played four times. The first was an away game at Winchelsea, where the wind was so strong that no one wanted to bowl into it – so I did. It blew from third man to wide mid-on; the ball swirled around wonderfully, and I took six cheap wickets.

Next we went to Jevington, a village of about twenty souls; they played in a field, with a tin shack for a pavilion. My first over went for eighteen, including two sixes; we had to find the ball in a clump of trees. After that, in three more overs I took six wickets for one run, including another hat-trick. In the last two games I took ten more wickets, so I finished the season with 22, at an average of under five.

Back in Cambridge for a year, I decided to ignore college cricket and play for Whittlesford. You could eat a disgusting amount of tea for a shilling; the annual subscription was only fifteen. They awarded caps for fifties or hat-tricks; I soon took a hat-trick in a beer match (they seemed to come quite easily just then), but declined the cap, saying that I would take a proper one later. Of course I never did.

It was at Sutton that I really learned to bowl. Sutton was in the newly-formed Surrey League, and played serious cricket. The league sides had a number of players who had been on county staffs; Bill Smith played for us for a while, after ten years with Surrey. There was even the odd Test cricketer, past or future: Russell Endean, the South African; David Hookes, before he became famous; John Emburey, kept out of the Middlesex side by Fred Titmus. In my second year Graeme Pollock played for us, but this was exceptional; he was playing for the (televised) International Cavaliers on a Sunday, and wanted to fill up his Saturdays.

Of course I was not a first team cricketer; I was not quick enough through the air to trouble good batsmen, nor was I quite accurate enough. I was also, in good cricket, a number eleven batsman and a poor fielder. I used to stand at mid-on, the duffers' position, and no one thought of moving me. (I was a *specialist* mid-on, I said.) But I played a number of games for the Sunday firsts, and just twice for the Saturday league side; in one of these games I took wickets, having been promoted from the thirds overnight.

It was surprising how, in many ways, it was easier to bowl for the first team than the third. I had a number of variations: a quicker leg-break, a little in-swinger which usually dropped too short, another leg-break which drifted in to the batsman and sometimes hit him on the toe. But I never had a googly. Good batsmen, however, would spend two or three overs looking for it, which gave me a little leeway. Then there was the fielding. For first teams I would bowl on or outside the off stump with six men on the off; six off-side attacking shots might produce one four and five good stops. Third team fielders, however, simply trundled after the ball and fetched it back from the boundary. (Against lowlier teams I had an extra man on the leg; they hit across the line more.) There was the catching, and the wicket-keeping; I was very dependent on my keepers, as I took a lot of wickets with stumpings.

My three Surrey League wickets came from two good stumpings and a startling catch.

I learnt, from different captains, about field placings. I learnt from bowling long spells; once I bowled twenty-three overs (the concentration goes, rather than the energy). I learned how to bowl to different sorts of batsmen. It was all very fascinating. The social mix was good, too; I talked to all sorts of people I would not otherwise have met.

Some of them were rather distinguished. I played with or against three Test cricketers in my time at Sutton, two of whom were pre-war. The first was Bertie Clarke, who had come over with the 1939 West Indians as a teenage leg-spinner; thirty years later, he was still taking wickets for the BBC. Then there was Roy Swetman, briefly an England wicket-keeper. Between spells with Surrey, Notts and Gloucestershire, he would play for Banstead. Ken Ohlson, Sutton second team captain and later a Surrey committee member, told me he was 'a proper little outsider'. He did not keep for Banstead; he scored a lot of runs and did some bowling. He treated me quite kindly, using his feet and pushing me around for ones and twos.

Finally there was Arthur Wellard; I played with him in Sutton cricket week when he was seventy. He insisted on batting number eleven, though Jim Barnard and I, real number elevens, were both in the side. He would walk singles, fairly slowly. He had been a notable hitter; he hit an off-spinner over mid-on for four, and when mid-on was pushed back to the boundary, cleared him with a six. Then he was bowled, playing back. "After the first two," he said, "I thought the next one would be shorter"; but it wasn't.

His bowling was a revelation. He was desperately keen to take wickets. "Polish the ball," he said to me (I was bowling at the other end), "polish the ball!" I had never polished the ball; I never needed to. He walked up six or seven paces; the arm was slightly bent, though no one said anything. He bowled an inner, an outer, an off-break, a queer high-tossed thing which had people playing early. He got through twenty-odd overs and took three for forty-something. The rest of the time he stood very fine at first slip. He was still in the bar at eleven p.m.; I left him to it.

❖

I stopped playing when I was about thirty-five. The children were growing up and it was taking a lot of time, and I had also suffered from a sort of virus which left me with less energy. I enjoyed being there, but the zip had gone. So I became a watcher.

I had the good fortune to see Brian Lara's 375 in Antigua, in 1994. In the previous Test he had looked like a sort of West Indian Gower: bound to give pleasure to a lot of people, but likely to get out any time. In Antigua, it was quite different; he had clearly set himself a task, and the result looked fairly inevitable. He played two streaky shots at the end of the second day, by which time he had already topped 300; otherwise there was barely a blemish until he was in sight of the record, when he suddenly became rather nervous, and had to be calmed down by young Chanderpaul. The only place to bowl to him, I decided, was up into his armpit.

Sometimes Test matches can look strangely familiar. I was at the Oval when Tufnell took 6 for 29 against the 1992 West Indians. They went mad; they came down the wicket and were bowled or stumped, or holed out at mid-off. I have occasionally induced this sort of suicide in village cricket, just by tossing the ball up. In the second innings they played him sensibly, and he took 0 for 160.

And sometimes I am carried right back to prep school

– by Test batsmen who are run out through not grounding their bats, or through colliding in mid-pitch. My old headmaster would not have approved. The striker, he insisted, should run towards the bowler's side; the non-striker should run down the other side. It makes sense.

Once I wrote a leg-break poem, one of three Cricket Songs published in my *Unfashionable Song* (1991). David Frith reviewed this briefly for *Wisden Cricket Monthly* (he also printed the poem), and the MCC library bought a copy; later, they reprinted the other two poems in an MCC anthology (*A Breathless Hush*). The attitudes of the leg-break poem are rather 1980s; it was before the days of Shane Warne, or even Ian Salisbury. My Uncle, Graham Hough, liked it; by now, he was a Cambridge Professor of English. It was probably the last thing of mine he saw, as his sight went after that.

Elegy

I gave my life to leg-breaks;
I tossed them high and slow.
The skipper, he's a modern man
And doesn't want to know.

Only a gentle shuffle
As fingers bite and twist;
The art's in feigned simplicity,
The power is from the wrist.

But here's containing off-spin,
And here's a bunch of quicks,
And high and slow the sun may go
From here to half past six

Before he calls me over.
Oh, grant me again, dear God,
The teasing flight that pitches right,
That beats the forward prod

With easy spin; then dig me in
Content beneath the sod.

Of course one wanted to take wickets as well. But in another sense, beating the bat was enough; it was an aesthetic experience. I think if I could have played cricket like squash – forty minutes bowling a week, say, just for the sake of it – I would have gone on a lot longer.

My last game of any description was with Guildford Cathedral Choir, Decani v Cantoris; I dismissed the organist, Andrew Millington, with my final delivery. My last bowl of all was on the s.s. Oriana, of all places, in 1996; Westminster Abbey Choir sang at the launch (*The Triumphs of Oriana*). We discovered a cricket net on the top deck, and I bowled several overs. But I shall not do it again.

Six

MORE FAMILY

I MUST not forget Wicked Uncle Sam. Sam was not a blood relation; he was married to Father's Aunt Lil. He was a ship's purser, and (I think) had a wife in more than one port. Having spent what little money Aunt Lil had, he disappeared. However, when Lil's father died, he turned up at the funeral. "You're not welcome here, Sam," Archie told him. (Archie, it has to be said, had been sleeping with Lil.) But Sam knew what he was about. Aunt Lil, as an abandoned wife with children, was left more in the will than her siblings and, like a fool, she took him back. Of course he spent her money again, and disappeared a second time, for good. Father remembered him as the most generous of uncles. We still have the christening spoon he gave to Father, a little mangled by a waste disposal unit of Mother's (the sort of thing chic kitchens had in the 1960s). It is an interesting relic.

For years, Father used to stay with us in the summer to watch a day of the Oval Test match. He, Tristram and I went together – three generations. The day followed a ritual pattern. After an hour and a half's play he would announce that he was going for a walk, which meant that he was going for a drink; he would return after forty minutes or so, in time for our sandwich lunch. For the first hour after lunch he was more or less asleep. "Haven't seen much of Gilbert lately," he announced one year, at about three o'clock. Gilbert, a rather undistinguished Australian fast bowler, had been bowling for the previous hour. On the way home he would buy flowers for Janet. "I've had a lovely life," he told me on one of these occasions; and yet I sometimes wonder if he was not a slightly disappointed man.

Father became chairman of the firm in 1952, and when six years later Archie moved down to Sussex, he must finally have felt in charge. But times were changing. Ours was a smallish firm, and in order to survive you had to be bigger. In 1961 four companies, of which the largest were ours and Harrisons of Leicester, joined up to become Associated Seed Merchants, Ltd. (or Asmer). Robert Kershaw, the head of Harrisons, became chairman, with the idea that Father would succeed him in the following year; but somehow this never happened. Robert was a financial man; Father was more of a true seedsman. Perhaps he would not have been a good chairman. I am sure, however, that this disappointment was partly behind Mother and Father's rather surprising move to Essex in 1965. They bought an old thatched house called Hawkins Harvest, with twenty acres. Father continued to draw his full director's salary for a while; but in fact he had semi-retired.

In due course Martin became chairman of Asmer – and found that he had inherited problems. The founders, and one or two others who joined later, had all wanted to hang on to their own little patch, which was proving uneconomic. Properties had to be sold and people made redundant; it was a painful time. Finally, in the early 1980s, it was decided to sell out. Asmer was bought by some Americans. They wanted a quick return for their money (they did not understand the seed business) and soon sold the firm on, in several pieces. The firm had gone from nothing to nothing, in about one hundred and twenty years, and Father had watched its demise. Though in another sense, this was his salvation.

Mother and Father had fourteen happy years at Hawkins Harvest. The house was Mother's preserve (she loved houses); outside there were lawns, flowers, vegetables, a wood, a bog-garden. Mother kept ducks on the pond. They got to know their neighbours. Up the road were two very ancient ladies, the Miss Hooles. "Of course we always liked dear Mr. Gladstone," one of them said. A little farther away was Edward Barron's smallholding; Edward helped with the gardening, and became a friend. On Christmas morning there was champagne for the locals, an occasion Uncle Graham referred to as 'the tenants' ball'.

But all was not quite what it seemed. By 1979 they could no longer afford to live at Hawkins, and they moved to a smaller house called Long Acre, overlooking a farmer's field.

Five years later, just before their golden wedding, came the revelation; Father, it appeared, had almost no money at all.

How had this come about? Partly, it was the result of the very high inflation of the 1970s, for which he had not allowed. Charles Pomfret, Father's cousin and the firm's accountant, once suggested that he had made some rather foolish share dealings. But much of it, I think, was a refusal to face unpleasant facts, and a continuing to spend money which was not really there. I suspect that spending money, and being seen to do so, was important to his self-esteem, which had suffered years of battering from his own father.

They sold Long Acre and moved to a wooden bungalow in Morcott, Rutland, in order to be near Martin. Mother called it Lowood, after a childhood home.

And then, like a fairy story, everything changed. We all had shares in the firm; Mother and Father had rather a lot. For some years, these had paid no dividend, but with the American takeover they were suddenly valuable. At a stroke, Father became comparatively wealthy. Something had turned up.

But of course Mother must have felt let down, and Father must have known that she did. She also increasingly disapproved of his drinking (she did not drink at all, because of her digestion). Father's sherry-pouring was famous. He was a generous host, and his sherry glasses were large – but his was the largest. His first move was to fill his own glass and down it in one; then he would start on the real first round. Very late in life he suffered from late-onset diabetes, brought on entirely by drinking, which Mother regarded as shameful.

No doubt many of us will go batty over something; Father went batty over money. Now that I am retired myself, I can understand some of his other problems. His retirement on full pay was seen as a cunning move by some, but with almost no interests other than the seed trade, it left him (apart from gardening) with not enough to do. It also left him without a sufficient sense of self-importance. His retirement was long, and perhaps a little empty; he had not really thought it through. And yet – "I have had a lovely life"; and in many ways it was true.

Father and Mother were utterly different. Father was not remotely taciturn; much of the time, he was rather jolly. But though he had strong feelings, he was not articulate about them, and he had a secretive side. Mother, on the other hand, told us anything and everything. I knew all about her courtship, Martin's adoption, her row with Grandfather, the difficulties surrounding my birth. She had firm opinions ("Perfectly ridiculous!" was a favourite phrase), and strong feelings of her own. There were people she liked, and people she disapproved of. Her life was very vivid to her, and we all knew what was in her mind.

There was the matter of their wills, for instance. Mother altered hers from time to time, discussing the changes as she went. Father had a strong sense of family, and we knew that he would not leave his money to the cats' home, but it was never mentioned. After he died, we found a curious little note, addressed 'To my Sons, Martin and Humphrey':

> In the event of any problems, financial or otherwise, on my decease, I rely on you both to take care of your mother to the best of your ability as good sons.

Given the date, 1st April 1981, this was clearly written during his financial troubles, of which none of us then knew anything.

Mother, too, kept tinkering with her proposed funeral service as though it were a work of art. She had almost no religious beliefs; she had been confirmed into the Church of England as an adult, but it never really took. However, she knew a tame vicar, who would give her the service she wanted. But he died, and after talking to other residents of her retirement home, she gave it up. "Do what you like," she said; "I shan't be there." We used as much as we could of the final draft. By contrast, I once heard Father say that, unlike Mother, he believed in an afterlife, but he never went to church in his later years, and if he had any ideas about his funeral, he kept them to himself.

I know more about Mother's family than Father's, because she talked about them more. After he died, we discovered family photographs and other documents of Father's which we had never seen. The subjects of some of the photos are irrecoverable; there is no one to ask.

Apart from a few months as secretary to her Uncle Otis, Mother never had a job. Her idea of marriage was to run the home, bring up the children and support her husband. (At that time it was almost everyone's idea; Mother's first live-in maid, for instance, stopped work as soon as she got married.) She slightly disapproved of both Martin's wives for not being sufficiently supportive. Virginia, it is true, went her own way – and had expensive tastes. Poor Jean got into trouble because she would not fly, and so could not accompany Martin on foreign business trips. Janet gave up work to have our two children, but soon started a nursery school in our house round Tristram, the younger of them; when he went to school, she returned to teaching. Mother was very fond of Janet, and admired her energy. She could also see that we were perfectly happy. But I think she felt that as a wife Janet was an interesting sort of freak; this was not how it was really done.

In her Formby years, Mother did welfare work for SSAFA, the Soldiers', Sailors' and Airmen's Families Association. (Some time after she died, I was amused to do a Special Service for SSAFA in Westminster Abbey.) Later, she took up spinning and weaving. She would buy whole fleeces, and convert them into rugs, bed-covers, scarves, gloves and other garments, mostly using the natural colours of the wool. For a while she sold to London shops –Harrods, Harvey Nichols, Cranks. She could not always supply the bulk orders they wanted. She also worked out that, in terms of pounds per hour, she could have made more money cleaning floors. But she was not doing it for the money; she enjoyed it. In the end, arthritis prevented her using the treadle of the spinning wheel; she tried an electric motor, but it was not the same.

Father and Mother moved into an old people's home together. Father did not want to go; he wanted to stay at Morcott and be looked after by Mother. But Mother was becoming more and more tired, Father did less and less, and it could not go on. Father never went to see their new home; the management had to take his existence on trust. He was not very interested in houses; when they had been to view Cartmel Lodge, he had mainly looked at the garden. He also knew that Mother would make him comfortable. But mostly he did not want to face it. He never settled there, and died within nine months. He was eighty-three.

Mother lived out her last years with great dignity. She was delighted to see me, but never fussed. "I am determined to enjoy myself," she would say; "it's such a waste if you don't." She had had two tragedies in her life; one was the death of her first baby, the other I shall come to. But she was quite clear that it was better to have had two awful things happen in an otherwise rather wonderful life than to have led a life which she would have described as 'dreary'. "I wouldn't have missed being alive for anything."

She faced death with great calmness. "It doesn't matter if I die tomorrow," she would say; "there's no one depending on me." She was interested in people to the last; she particularly enjoyed male company. In her final year she teamed up with an old doctor; they would sit together after lunch, and sometimes he came to tea. After she died, he was quite upset. "The last thing I expected," he told Martin, "was to fall in love again at my age." He was ninety and half blind, and can never really have seen her. She was not in love with him; he was just a friend.

She died very suddenly one night, just after I had visited her. She was eighty-five.

By the end of the summer of 1960, my brother Stuart was seventeen. He had passed three good 'A' levels and had won a place to read Languages at Christ's College, Cambridge. The 'gap' year had not really been invented then; however, it was decided quite sensibly that he should spend the intervening year in France and Germany.

There was no problem with the German leg. He spent two terms with a solid German family, going to school with his friend Hermann. Then he set off for Paris, where he was registered with a language school. Having spoken nothing but German for several months, his French was a little rusty; he was put in too low a class, and got bored. So he signed himself off.

He drifted round Paris, much of the time with two rather pleasant girls; one of them was the daughter of Hugh Gaitskell, the Labour politician. A directionless period in adolescence, I have since read, can be a cause of schizophrenia. Certainly it was after this that his troubles began.

In Cambridge, he soon switched from Languages to Anthropology. I saw little of him that year; we were in different colleges, and led different lives. But Mother, with an unerring maternal sense, knew that all was not well. She was regarded as a neurotic parent; but she was right.

He came home and was seen by psychiatrists. The cure was to spend a year away from Cambridge, resting his brain. He worked for Asmer.

After that, it was a see-saw. He went back to Cambridge, but was ill again by the end of the year. I remember Father describing his twenty-first birthday (I forget why I was not there). A room had been booked at the University Arms

Hotel, with dinner and dancing. But Stuart was past coping with invitations, and almost no one turned up. He failed his exams, though only just, and that was the end of his University career.

There were bad times, and better times. Once he took an overdose and had to be brought round. For a while he held down a steady job as a laboratory assistant in Cambridge. He got engaged; he and his fiancée stayed with us in Sutton. But he knew when the bad times were coming; he told her she would be better off without him, and signed himself back into Fulbourn, the grim Victorian mental hospital outside Cambridge. Three months later, he lay down on a railway line and let a train run over him. He was twenty-six.

Even at the worst, he was himself. After the overdose, he was in Addenbrooke's Hospital; Mother was with him when he came round. "Oh, am I in the *old* Addenbrooke's?" he said. "I thought I was in the nice new building." He spent his last afternoon helping his fellow-inmates at Fulbourn. I spoke to one of them at the funeral; "I'm his brother," I said. "We're all his brothers," he replied. It grieves me that I did so little for him.

It is difficult to know what he would have made of his life. At Cambridge, he joined the Footlights Club, the breeding ground for people like Jonathan Miller and Peter Cook. I have a programme of a Smoking Concert in which he took part; the chairman was Graham Garden, an old prep school friend, later to be one of The Goodies.

Staying with us one Christmas (his last, I think), he suddenly asked for a pair of scissors. He re-emerged after half an hour with a coloured cardboard caricature of me, singing; the arms and legs were attached by split pins which moved when you pulled a string. This was for Jonathan, aged two and a half. We still have it.

He was a one-off, and we loved him. It was a terrible waste.

After the demise of Asmer, my brother Martin became a consultant. He did a lot of work for British Tobacco, and was also part of a government quango which involved trips to Nigeria. He had had a distinguished life in the seed trade, for which he was eventually awarded the MBE. ("Quite right, too," said Father; "he should have had it years ago.") For a while he was President of the British section of the International Association of Plant Breeders, and later became President of the whole international body. (Mother rang up in great excitement. "Martin *was* President of just the British bit," she said; "now he's President of the Whole World.")

Martin was devoted to Mother and Father; it was he who looked after them in their old age. He managed their finances, visited them constantly, and found their retirement home in Ketton. Though he and Jean had wanted to move for years, he put it off so as not to upset them. Eventually they bought a house on Mersea Island, and settled Mother into a new home nearby, a Queen Anne building in spacious grounds.

I got to know him better after Mother's death; it brought us together. I had always telephoned Mother on Sunday nights; now I rang Martin. Once he came to a service in Westminster Abbey and, though quite unmusical, made a perceptive comment about Martin Neary, the choirmaster. "For someone who's supposed to be in charge," he said, "he seems to have to make an awful lot of fuss." Jonathan described him as a 'people person'.

He had moved to Mersea for the sailing. He had done his National Service in the navy, where he trained as a diver. Soon after, he was appointed to a job with Jacques

Cousteau, the underwater explorer, but turned it down in favour of the family business, because he thought he ought to. His sailing was serious. In his fifties, he and several others made a long voyage to Iceland. Jean telephoned while he was away; she had just heard Kipling's 'Harp Song of the Dane Women' on the radio.

> What is a woman that you forsake her,
> And the hearth-fire and the home-acre,
> To go with the old grey Widow-maker…

The sea – the old grey Widow-maker. I know from his log that there were dangerous moments. But he came back safely.

Quite late in life he got in touch with his biological family; he met his birth-mother twice before she died. She had been made pregnant by a rotter, who left her in the lurch. "At least you don't look like him," she said.

He died quite suddenly on his yacht, aged sixty-one. Driving down to see Jean, it occurred to me that someone ought to speak about his life at the funeral. A few miles further on, I realised that it would have to be me. Martin had always been there; he was a sort of buffer. Now, of the five of us, I was the only one left.

Seven

POETRY

POETRY CREPT up on me. It began in my second school, when I was encouraging the children to write; after a while, I thought I ought to be having a go myself. I did not really know what I was doing. My first more or less recognisable poems were little imagist lyrics. It was about this time that I met Peter Dale.

Peter was the leading light in a local poetry group. He had already published two books with Macmillan, and he laid down the law about everything. He gave the impression of being a great poet who was waiting for the world to recognise him; partly, I think, this covered a certain insecurity. He thought (quite rightly) that one ought to be able to justify every word. I once suggested that a sonnet of his was repetitive; "No, it isn't," he said. This was hardly justification, but it was difficult to argue with his tone. He also talked a lot about technique. Over the years I learnt which of his criticisms to accept, and which were the sort of thing he often said but which I never agreed with. I also learnt not to accept his amendments; the fault may have been real enough, but the amendment usually sounded more like him than me.

I struggled on. I wrote rather slowly, and threw a lot

away; I wrote when things came to me. This would never have done for a novel, say, or music, but for short poems it was not a bad idea; lyric poetry can never be a full-time job.

Peter was associate editor of a poetry magazine, *Agenda*; the main editor was William Cookson. William had written to Ezra Pound as a teenager, and visited him; he started the magazine as a tribute. He was a devoted Poundian; Pound was a substitute religion. Any item in the literary press criticising Pound – even for indefensible things like the wartime Rome broadcasts, or the anti-semitism – was sure of a reply from William. And any book Pound said was good *was* good; Gavin Douglas's *Virgil*, for instance, or Arthur Golding's *Ovid* ('the most beautiful book in the language'). Uncle Graham told me that he had visited Pound in St Elizabeth's, the hospital for the criminally insane in Washington; for a while he seemed quite normal, but then would come an outpouring of bile about Jews, and so on. The accepted view was that he was in St Elizabeth's as a kindness; the alternative would have been a trial for treason. But perhaps he was really bonkers. I read my way through Pound, of course, but except in odd snatches could not really see the point: the early stuff full of tiresome diction, and the Cantos rambling and requiring thousands of footnotes to elucidate their learning, which was not lightly worn.

Peter was no Poundian; he had other gods – the Shakespeare sonnets, for instance, and Edward Thomas. He and William would argue; over the years it became like a bad marriage. William was amiable and shambling, and a little unreliable; he looked rather like Dylan Thomas, though in fact he was descended from Wordsworth. He would quietly do exactly what he felt like, regardless of sense – publish a Romanian Poetry issue, for instance, because he happened to have a Romanian girlfriend at the time. When I became involved, *Agenda* was still quite vigorous, with a large Arts Council grant and a decent subscription list; it also paid at proper Arts Council rates. It still struggles on, but the steam has gone out of it.

Agenda published some of my earliest poems, and continued to support me over the years. I also reviewed for them; laying down the law was fun, and one learnt (slowly) to be responsible. I gave rather a cool review to Larkin's last book, *High Windows*; there were, inevitably, some good things in it, but Larkin was on the wane by then – as he himself knew. On the other hand, I praised sections of Ted Hughes' *Moortown*, rather against the grain, as Hughes was not much admired in *Agenda* circles – nor, particularly, by me. I tried to plug my enthusiasms; I wrote a long article on Ivor Gurney, for instance. Sometimes I gave myself a lot of work. Asked to review John Heath-Stubbs' three verse plays, I was forced to consider what the verse in verse drama is *for*, and what (apart from the Greeks and the Elizabethan/Jacobeans) is the tradition. I read my way through some of the nineteenth-century stuff (Keats' *King Otho*, Shelley's *The Cenci*), all of Yeats (not much there except *Purgatory*), Christopher Fry (better than I expected), Eliot, of course (effective in the set-pieces of *Murder in the Cathedral*, but hopeless at the naturalistic stuff). All this for a three-page review. (I once drove John Heath-Stubbs to a reading. He was rather like old blind Homer, except that he behaved as though he could still see; this was not a good idea when crossing roads. *Agenda* had turned down his long King Arthur poem, *Artorius* – quirky, but good in its way, and it *does* wear its learning lightly. They thought it was too literary; I thought they were mad.)

All of this was very stimulating. Peter and I would drive up after school to William's flat in Battersea; he cooked joints, slowly and well, and we would drink a lot. (William, it has to be said, had a problem with drink.) But before that, we opened the submissions. Most were hopeless, and could be rejected at a glance. Much of the time we printed half-way decent stuff because that was all there was. But very rarely one struck gold – a lovely poem I found called 'Jonson Grown Older', for instance, by Anne Haskins (of whom I otherwise know nothing), a sequel to 'Have you seen but a white lily grow'.

Peter's own poetry (I am looking back over thirty years) is rather variable, as is inevitable with someone who writes so much. There is a handful of really first-rate pieces, and a larger amount of good second-rate stuff. Third-rate Dale (it seems to me) is in no language that anyone ever wrote, thought or spoke, and uses odd shifts to achieve its rhymes, particularly in some of the translations. I find his Dante hard to read. On the other hand, I was fascinated to watch his sonnet sequence, *One Another*, emerge – one or two poems a day at one stage; and the finished result (it is about a marriage) is genuinely moving. There are other lyrics which I would not be without – 'A Time to Speak', from *Edge to Edge*, for instance.

Poets are self-taught; they expect to be. The only way is to read a lot, absorbing what has been done before and how it was done – in minute technical detail. At the same time one needs to write and write, being self-critical, open to others' criticism, revising a lot, throwing a lot away. One needs to weigh words, their shape and texture ('cow-parsley' is impossible – three heavy syllables). One needs to try things out (Auden's 'Lauds' looks interesting; I wonder if I could do it?). Peter's very conscious systems of rhyme and metre were a help. To an increasing extent one trusts one's instinct – but the instinct has to be trained. All of which seems obvious enough now, though at the time I had to discover it.

Of course one has to have something to write about; it helps to have a few obsessions. (Peter's are a little repetitive.) But when the Muse is really working, there is no distinction between form and content. Poems do not present themselves as ideas; they come as a line, a rhythm, a compulsion. One follows one's nose, and the shape is the poem; this is true even of poems in formal rhymes and stanzas. Of course some such poems, or parts of them, have to be very consciously made; but having written two or three sonnets (say), one gets into the flow, and begins to think in sonnet form.

The flow is important. Like anything else (playing tennis), one needs to keep in practice, and starting up after a long lay-off is difficult. The more one does, the easier it gets – until tiredness, or staleness, sets in. I remember sitting down after school to write one of my Winchester sonnets, knowing with absolute certainty that I would have it done by six o'clock, when they closed the building. At other times, it is a debilitating struggle.

My own literary gods were becoming clearer; the short lyric was the thing. Wyatt I had loved since Cambridge ('My lute awake', 'They flee from me that sometime did me seek'). Then there was Campion, a gentler and more vulnerable spirit ('Kind are her answers, / But her performance keeps no day, / Breaks time as dancers / From their own music when they stray…'). Campion, who wrote his own music for his lyrics, and I have no idea which came first. Certainly the verbal rhythms are unique, the musical ones rather plain. (Could he not *hear* this?) Like Peter, I revered the best of the Shakespeare sonnets, but also some of the lyrics. 'O mistress mine' is almost a collection of clichés, and I can imagine him knocking it off in ten minutes; but it is also quite wonderful – and desperately sad. Nash's 'In Time of Plague' ('Brightness falls from the air…'), Herbert's 'Virtue', Waller's 'Go, lovely rose', were touchstones. (Graham, wondering in about 1960 what 'cool' meant in its new, colloquial sense, was told that 'Go, lovely rose' was a 'cool' poem. The word has moved on again since.) Then there was Hardy. There is far too much Hardy; he was unbelievably clumsy, and not remotely self-critical. He had genius, but no talent. The genius emerges in the few really great poems ('At Castle Boterel', 'During Wind and Rain' – 'Down their carved names the rain-drop ploughs...'), and in the unfakeable personality which shines through. Technical brilliance is not enough (a good thing in Hardy's case); you need the sense of a man talking to men. Herbert has it – and Larkin. The best of Larkin ('At Grass', 'An Arundel Tomb') is in my bones. After the publication of the letters, with their evidence of racism, misogyny, philandering, he was reviled by poets not fit to lick his boots – Donald Davie, Tom Paulin (a polemicist ass). My love for Housman came later.

Of course I was not only published in *Agenda*; there were plenty of magazines around. For some years, sending out submissions and receiving rejection slips or (less often) acceptances was part of life. Sometimes one had tapped the wrong market; the magazine did not do my sort of thing. At others, one got caught up in the bitter rivalries which, in retrospect, are one of the more amusing aspects of the scene: *X* would not publish me because I was published by *Y*. (Peter, a conspiracy theory man, was full of these notions.)

In 1975 I achieved two small pamphlets. Roland John lived in Sutton. He was a fairly inept poet; he could not even punctuate (neither could Byron, but his publisher did it for him). He was another Poundian; in due course he and William both published guides to *The Cantos*. Peter Dent was an old school friend of Peter Dale's; he wrote free verse lyrics so attenuated and allusive that one sometimes had little idea of what they were about. He thought that rhymes and scansion led to insincerity. Roland and Peter Dent both started poetry presses; Roland's was small and ongoing, Peter's tiny and ephemeral. When each of them asked for a booklet, I divided my better lyrics into two heaps (a sequence for Dent, random ones for Roland). There was a smattering of reviews in obscure places. I had begun.

It took till 1982 for my first real book to appear. By this time I had a more solid body of verse, and had learned some new tricks. There were sonnets, a ballad, a villanelle, other sorts of rhymed stanzas, and the Auden 'Lauds' repeated-line thing. There was blank verse and free verse. I tried unrhymed tetrameters, which was supposed to be unviable. There were two translations from Horace (I had previously done a lot of Catullus, to which I shall return). One of the Horace, *O fons Bandusiae*, I had first come across as a bored teenager; my Latin master took us over and over it one hot afternoon. Six months later he was dead. I am sure now that he was having a last look.

I called the book *Gods and Mortals*. The classical influence predominated; there are poems about Odysseus, and Circe, Actaeon, and Cinna the poet (the unluckiest man in history: praised by Catullus, killed in mistake for someone else, and not a line of his verse survives). But it was not only the literature; I was involved, in an amateur sort of way, with the whole classical world. I was edging back towards Christianity; in the meantime, one of the attractions of paganism was its sense of the numinous in the everyday.

A whole sonnet sequence was the result of a commission from the then Dean of Winchester, Michael Stancliffe. 1979 marked the nine hundredth anniversary of the foundation of the Norman cathedral. I was singing a lot with the cathedral choir at the time, and we did everything that year: concerts, broadcasts, a Royal Maundy service, a three-week tour of the U.S.A. Michael Stancliffe, as a private venture of his own, decided to commission a book of poems from various hands; having come across my name in *Agenda*, he approached me. I think he wanted a single poem, but I misunderstood and did five, starting with Cenwalh, the founder of the first Saxon cathedral, and finishing with William Walker, the diver who spent seven years underpinning the foundations in the early 1900s. A friend described them as tourist poems, but I rather liked them; I thought they had a fluidity within the form which I had not managed before. (Michael Stancliffe did beautiful lettering, rather like David Jones, the Welsh poet and artist much admired by William. I still have one of his envelopes.)

Then came the reviews. One of the more interesting was from Dick Davis, quite a good poet in a miniaturist sort of way. He was a fellow-Kingsman, but younger than I; I had never met him. He wrote:

> ...the poems are not to be faulted, but they are calculatedly unambitious. I am sure that Clucas would infinitely prefer to write a good minor poem ... than to botch an attempt at the nebulously 'great work' ...

Janet and Tristram agreed that this was how I was.

Ten or twelve years later, during a dull sermon in Westminster Abbey, a colleague passed me the novel he was reading; he had been struck by mention of a couple of swans called Humphrey and Janet. The novel was *The Chymical Wedding*, by Lindsay Clarke. The author was a Kingsman; he looked from his photograph to be about my age. Perhaps he had borrowed our names.

Of course I read it. A principal character, Alex Darken, was a poet and a Cambridge graduate. He had published two slim volumes, followed by writer's block. He had also translated Catullus, and was about to give up teaching.

This, in about 1990, was exactly my position. As to his verse, it was 'intact and chinkless – too guardedly so, according to at least one reviewer' – which sounded very like the Davis review. I wrote to Lindsay Clarke; he had never heard of us, and his Alex Darken was based on – Dick Davis.

Literary coincidence struck first in the early 1970s. I was walking round the Roman walls of Chester with the family; then we went into W.H.Smith's. In a random fashion, and from a miscellaneous heap, I bought Henry James' *The Ambassadors*. By page twelve, two of the characters are walking round the Roman walls of Chester. There have been further coincidences, equally striking; they no longer surprise me. They do not seem to mean anything.

One rather delightful spin-off of the Winchester sonnets was a poetry reading. I quite enjoy them; compared with singing, talking to people is a doddle. They are not really what poetry is about, but they spread the word. This, though, was the only one I have done in the north transept of a cathedral, and with a bishop as fellow-reader. Bishop John Taylor was quite a good poet, and a contributor to Michael Stancliffe's book. He rang up; he was worried that he might not have enough material. But I was out, and it was Janet who explained that you were allowed to chat between the poems. We had supper in the Bishop's Palace first: "a sausage and a lettuce leaf," said Mrs. Taylor. They were unassuming people.

My Catullus translations were published later than *Gods and Mortals*, but mostly written earlier. One day in about 1975, I pulled the Loeb *Catullus* off the shelf, and pitched in. Not knowing the difficulties made it easier. But they are considerable.

Latin metre is based on length, English on stress, so one cannot really give an impression of what the Latin sounds like. One can substitute stress for length, of course; but there is no history in English of Latin forms such as Sapphics, or elegiac couplets. For a minor versifier, working in a fixed tradition is relatively easy; working in the dark is rather more difficult. Alternatively, one can use standard English verse forms; but then one will have lost a lot of Catullus.

The most successful translations are one-offs. Housman's *Diffugere nives* (Horace) is masterly; Milton's attempt to do *Quis multa gracilis* into the original metre is a curiosity.

Campion and Ben Jonson both had a go at Catullus' *Vivamus, mea Lesbia*. (Campion: 'Heavens' great lamps do dive / Into their west, and straight again revive'; Jonson: 'Suns that set may rise again'.) But Campion sets off on his own after verse one, with Catullus' *Nox est perpetua una dormienda* as a sort of chorus line, and Jonson is more imitation than translation.

All of this, of course, I discovered gradually. My Latin was never very good. Apart from the Loeb crib, I was armed (eventually) with a dictionary, two different editions with commentaries (one of them missed out the dirty bits), two or three books on Catullus and several other people's translations. I used blank verse, unrhymed tetrameters, various sorts of free verse. Occasionally I tried to suggest Latin metres, without too strictly imitating them. I did whatever occurred to me or seemed to work at the time. I did *Attis*, for instance (one of Catullus' few longer poems), into a sort of English hexameter – just to see how it went.

Translation is a form of commentary, a way of reading the text. Had my Latin been better, I perhaps would not have felt the need. I translated as many as I wanted (perhaps two-thirds), and then stopped. Fellow-poets wondered why I chose Catullus at all; he had been done so often, and I could have made my mark with something more obscure. Later, I was rebuked for not finishing the job. Like William, I had gone my own way.

Graham wrote. 'What I find good in your versions,' he said, 'is that they are extremely close (they really *are* accurate translations) and at the same time the language is extremely pure and straightforward and natural – not translationese.' To be taken seriously by Graham (who had a sharp tongue) was rather delightful. There were some nice reviews; I particularly enjoyed the one which said 'Mr. Clucas's *Attis* is a triumph almost as awesome as its original'. But we did not sell very many copies – even now there are rather a lot left – and the book seemed doomed to oblivion.

Ten years after it came out, and twenty after I began it, I received a letter from Oxford University Press: could they use one of my versions in *The Oxford Book of Classical Verse in English Translation*? Of course they could. And there I was, with all the greats: Marlowe's *Ovid*, Dryden's *Virgil*, Pope's *Homer* – and Clucas's *Catullus*. A lot of less-than-greats, too, of course.

It got better. Three years later, Penguin Books wrote; they wanted no less than six of my versions for the Penguin Classics *Catullus in Translation*. The plan of the book was that every poem should appear in at least one version, and some of them in several. *Carmen* 56, for instance, was entrusted solely to me; 48 appeared in three versions, by me, Byron and Lovelace. This was my proper company, I felt. Finally, and very recently, Constable, the publishers, wrote; they were bringing out a biography of Catullus by Aubrey Burl, and wanted to print my translations as an appendix. Perhaps I had been along the right lines after all.

But poetry, somehow, was running out on me. By the mid-1980s I knew that there would be a second book, but no more. I can remember the exact moment, struggling by a river with a poem which would not come, when I told myself: "There's no law which says I have to do this."

Why it was, I cannot say. Graham told me once that the poetic impulse dies as one gets older and stops falling in love. I do not think that this was my case. I did not give poetry up; it gave me up. At about this period I began writing music again; for several years I was doing both at once. I suppose one took over from the other, though it did not feel like that at the time.

My second book, *Unfashionable Song*, came out in 1990, though none of it was written later than 1987. Roland John published it; Harry Chambers' Peterloo Press had done *Gods and Mortals*, but he declined the second book. There are things in it I like: some School Songs, some Cricket Songs, a villanelle which uses a Dowland song as one of its repeating lines, an Odysseus sequence, using Scottish landscape, which no one but me seemed to fancy very much. But perhaps it is a slightly thin book. Certainly it is no advance on its predecessor.

One poem had a curious genesis. I had tentatively begun the Winchester sonnets with one about a cold and bibulous organist; he was fictional, but perhaps I was remembering Thomas Weelkes, of Chichester. When the sequence turned out to be about real people, I cannibalised the sestet for a different poem and otherwise abandoned it. But I still had these eight lines. Not wanting to waste them, I concocted a new sestet one afternoon, and sent it off to a competition. It came first, and there was a nice cash prize.

Which leaves my Housman. My interest in A.E.H. began in a quiet way in the 1980s, with a reading of the Richard Graves biography. From time to time I have these obsessions, with writers or composers; some are quite minor and passing. This was major. It was a combination, briefly, of the ache and longing in the poetry (the 'No more' theme), the sadness of the life, and the man's wonderful ear. I read and re-read the poems, and everything else I could. I combed bibliographies, and got obscure things from libraries and second-hand dealers. I discovered the Housman Society, and went to one of its dinners; here were fellow-enthusiasts, and a Journal to write for.

My first two articles were a consideration of *The Name and Nature of Poetry* (Housman's 1933 lecture), and a brief, almost spoof-scholarly piece connecting Housman with Valentin Haussmann, the sixteenth-century Saxon composer. (I had come across him on an Abbey choir tour; Bob Lynn, my host in Houston, Texas, was a world expert.) In it, I took P.G.Naiditch to task for making two tiny errors. P.G.Naiditch had arrived on the scene several journals earlier; he was an American scholar who, like Housman, was fiercely scornful of factual error in others. He sounded terrifying. A minor point of my piece was whether there is one 'n' in Haussmann or two; the Journal editor, alas, sent no proofs, and blithely used either spelling at random. To impute error to P.G.Naiditch was amusing; to be at the same time apparently guilty myself was dreadful. I wrote to him.

Thus began a long and fascinating correspondence. At the height of my Housman-scholar period, I once told someone that 'I knew everything about Housman'. I probably did know most of what there was to know, but Naiditch, biographically and bibliographically speaking, really did know everything. I tried things out on him; I leant on him for advice. His replies, from the University College of Los Angeles, were long, detailed, prompt and courteous. There is some doubt about when A.E.H. first met Grant Richards, his eventual publisher; they give conflicting accounts. I reviewed the evidence, sorted it out to my satisfaction, and sent the result to Paul. His reply began: 'There are matters of which you are unaware...' I never published the article.

Once I met him; on a later Abbey tour, I found myself in Los Angeles with a free evening. He never mentioned the tour; we were straight into Housmania. He had books from Housman's library, with A.E.H.'s marginal notes. Another had marginalia by Gibbon. I wish I had kept a record; the details have gone dim.

But this was later. Following my nose, I had made one or two discoveries. A four-page extract exists of a talk on Matthew Arnold which Housman gave to the University College, London, Literary Society. When, exactly, was it given? From internal evidence, two authorities (one of them Naiditch) had suggested 'between October 1893 and July 30, 1894'. But I was unhappy with this. There was a reference (no matter why) to high scores made by Stoddart against the Australians; but Stoddart was not notable for such things until the Australian summer of 1894-95. Having also fixed on a new end-date, from references to Mr. Gladstone and Archdeacon Farrar, I came down firmly for the first two terms of 1895. Paul Naiditch agreed that I was probably right.

In his undergraduate years, Housman owned the *Poems and Romances* by the rather dim Victorian poet, G.A.Simcox; great chunks were transcribed into his commonplace book. Norman Marlow and Tom Burns Haber had already been over this ground, but I thought I ought to read Simcox for myself. I found a few faint pre-echoes of Housman not previously noted, and one rather remarkable one: 'the land of lost Delight'. 'The land of lost content' is one of Housman's most famous phrases; how had Marlow and Haber not spotted this?

Then there was Witter Bynner. Bynner was a rather third-rate American poet, and a Housman fan; they corresponded. Bynner sent Housman his first book of verse, with a request that Housman should be the dedicatee; Housman declined. The book contains three poems which are startlingly like three of Housman's. One has the same title, 'The Deserter'.

High is the fife and low the drum,
And people lean to see,
And hats are off when heroes come,
And none are off to me.

Housman or Bynner? Bynner, as it happens. Yet Bynner had almost certainly not seen Housman's 'The Deserter' by then, or the other two poems; and neither man referred to the coincidences, then or later.

Minor stuff, of course; but I was essentially an amateur, and the major work had, in any case, all been done.

Having put several articles together, it occurred to me that I had the basis for a book. I wrote a long piece explaining my Housman obsession, and another rather speculatively linking texts by Housman, Hardy, Scott, Burns, and a ghost story by M.R.James. (Had anyone previously noticed that Scott had written a *queer* novel?) Housman, prompted by Bynner, had admired the sonnets of the American F.G.Tuckerman; so I wrote about Tuckerman. I did a piece on Housman's blunders, and another on Housman and Westminster Abbey. (As a teenager, he had heard an anthem by Maurice Greene in the Abbey; I discovered which it was.) I wrote about Housman's 'For My Funeral', uncovering its sources and elucidating its strategies. The final piece was about Housman biography; I compared him, not very originally, with Larkin. In an appendix, I printed my own song-setting of 'Into my heart an air that kills'.

It was a small and eccentric book, published, rather oddly, by Salzburg University Press, which had an English Studies department. Producing it was a new experience. Everything was read by Paul Naiditch, and most of it by several other people. As a result I made amendments, perhaps a few too many; qualifications can deflect the line of one's thought. For permission to quote, I had to apply to the Society of Authors, guardians of the Housman literary estate, and also to the University of Texas at Austin. I wrote, too, to the Dorset County Museum; they held several Housman letters to Hardy which, amazingly, had never been published. The inter-library loans service was invaluable; Bynner's edition of Tuckerman came from the University of Hull – Larkin's old library. For Housman's *Thirty Letters to Witter Bynner*, I had to go to the Bodleian.

Not only was the book small, but so was the edition, and the press was obscure. There was a silly muddle about the distribution. But it got to the places which mattered. Paul's *Problems in the Life and Writings of A.E.Housman* refers to it as an authority. Archie Burnett's monumental and definitive edition of *The Poems of A.E.Housman* (O.U.P., 1997) includes it in the bibliography, and cites it in no less that four footnotes; Janet at one time thought that I was prouder of this than almost anything else. I was even able to point out an error to Mr. Burnett (not merely a misprint, of which there are several).

My book came out in 1996, to mark the centenary of the publication of *A Shropshire Lad*. There were a number of celebrations that year; I attended Housman conferences, for instance, in Bromsgrove and Ludlow. There was also the election of A.E.H. to Poets' Corner.

I had written to the Dean (Michael Mayne) about this soon after I arrived at the Abbey; admission to Poets' Corner is in the Dean's gift. Then I met Jack Bates. Jack Bates was a wartime Irish Guards officer and late-flowering academic, who would sometimes drop in to Abbey evensong on the way to regimental dinners. He, too, had written to the Dean about Housman. Pursuing it further, he discovered that what one needed was a series of testimonials from distinguished people: poets, scholars (literary and classical in Housman's case), politicians. He set to work. I gave a little advice; it was I who suggested

Seamus Heaney, for instance, since I knew that the Dean admired him.

His eventual list was impressive: Kingsley Amis, Heaney, Ted Hughes, Stephen Spender, John Bayley and Iris Murdoch, Roy Hattersley, Roy Jenkins, Enoch Powell – and many others. Enoch Powell, of course, was a classicist, an ex-Fellow of Trinity, and a former colleague of Housman's. I was amused that Jack included my own original letter along with the rest.

Poets' Corner had run out of space, and any further names were to be placed on lozenges in a newly-designed window. The Dean decided to begin with some obvious omissions: Pope, Herrick, Oscar Wilde. "I can't announce Wilde and Housman together," he told me. "Two homosexuals – the papers would get onto it. I thought of Wilde and Pope. Pope wasn't queer, was he? Was there a Mrs. Pope?" And then: "I'm sure previous deans didn't have to worry about this sort of thing."

The ceremony was in the hands of the Housman Society. Ian Bostridge sang; Alan Bennett gave an address. But the preceding evensong I planned myself. For the introit, we sang Housman's 'For My Funeral', to the Bach chorale which was used at his own funeral in Trinity College Chapel. The canticles were to *Stanford in C*, on the grounds that, of all the Stanford services, this was the one written when Housman and Stanford were colleagues at Trinity. For the anthem, we did Wesley's *Thou wilt keep him in perfect peace*; Housman would have heard it as a pall-bearer at Thomas Hardy's Abbey funeral. I insisted on the Authorised Version, contrary to the Abbey's current practice. I also, to amuse myself, put down my own Responses; no one queried it.

A slightly later celebration was Tom Stoppard's play, *The Invention of Love*, with Housman as protagonist. "Got the *Pink 'Un*?" Moses Jackson asks, somewhere in Act One.

"Good man. How were the Australians doing?" It was supposed to be 1885; but there was no Australian cricket team in England that year. I wrote to Sir Tom. '... I knew about the Australians,' he replied, 'and for that matter about the *Pink 'Un* not being in existence until a little later – this is the great thing about "memory plays" – the memory can be inaccurate. The play has a couple of dozen such misrememberings...' It was not, I thought, one of his better plays; but he was always clever.

And slowly I found that I was putting Housman behind me. Like Catullus, he was internalised, he was all there – but now I could move on, forgetting, of course, a lot of the detail. There were new obsessions: the novels of Charlotte M.Yonge, the operettas of Franz Lehar, Shostakovitch string quartets.

And little by little, I stopped reading poetry altogether. Losing interest as a practitioner was part of it; but I no longer seemed to feel the need. It is there if I want it, I know which the best poems are, and I have strong feelings about word setting. Occasionally I make a discovery – the Australian Gwen Harwood, for instance; but I have ceased to be curious. I do not know why. There is, I suppose, a limit to the number of things one can do properly, and at the same time.

Eight

SINGING (I)

I CANNOT remember a time when I was unable to sing; no doubt I shall come to it. Until quite late in life I had little teaching, and what I had was fairly ineffective; as with other things, I am largely self-taught.

I left Cambridge with a light tenor of slightly limited range, and a certain arrogance; King's choral scholars knew they were good. In our Bexhill years, Janet played for me a lot: *Die Schone Mullerin, Dichterliebe,* Brahms, Fauré, Duparc, English song. But we did little in public. I remember two recitals in schools; at one, we did a song of my own and the rather polite girls all said "Encore!" I do not think it was spontaneous.

During my Cambridge education year, I did the evangelist part in one of the Schutz passions, the Brahms *Liebeslieder* for Uppingham School, and there was the Madrigal Society. But I did much more singing when we moved to Sutton.

We arrived early in June, and my teaching did not begin until late September; the intervening period was for putting the house straight. But I could not do with the thought of four months' unrelieved decorating, so I decided to do an LRAM in Singing (Performing). The syllabus looked quite straightforward; Janet accompanied the songs, and the only training I had was a little Italian pronunciation from a non-musical bowls-playing friend of her father's. The paperwork was set on the assumption that singers were thick, and so was the sight-reading – eight bars of simple tune. "What about words?" I asked. "Oh, sing it to 'Ah'." "And tempo?" "You do it at any speed you can manage, dear." This was Olive Groves, once a noted contralto. Of course I passed. I have sometimes told people that I have 'no musical qualification beyond Grade Five Theory'; I tend to forget about my LRAM.

I also joined the Louis Halsey Singers. Louis, having founded the Elizabethan Singers, had somehow contrived to be thrown out by them, and had started again under his own name. He was one of those amiable conductors (there are lots of them) who collect quite competent people around them, so the results never sound too bad. I also sang for his professional group, the Thames Chamber Choir. I did a little with John Eliot Gardiner's Monteverdi Choir, which was amateur in those days, but I did not get on with him; there was a muddle about my availability, and I soon left. It made me a member of a fairly large club; he was always falling out with people.

I also built up a sort of solo career. Just before the age of thirty, something happens to a voice; it grows, with little apparent effort on one's own part. I found that I could do things which had been beyond me before. I gradually acquired a regular round of schools and choral societies; I perhaps did half a dozen solo jobs each winter. There were *Messiahs*, of course, but also *Creations*, the Mozart *Requiem*, Mozart and Haydn Masses (too many *Nelson* Masses – an unrewarding tenor part). Hinchley Wood School, under John Sutton, did an annual choral concert in those days, and I almost always did their tenor solos. (I baulked at the Verdi *Requiem*). One year it was *Elijah*, with Thomas Allen in the name part; he had been at college with John. It was for Hinchley Wood that I did my first *St John Passion*. It was hard work; I spent weeks floating around at the top of the voice, and singing little else. Baroque pitch had not been invented then. I have a tape of that performance (though not of later, better ones); it is quite respectable. I did *Matthew Passion* arias for John, too, with a different choir. I never did *St John* arias (the second one is a pig), or the *St Matthew* evangelist; I was never asked to. But I several times did things (the *St John Passion*, a particularly foul Bach cantata) just to see whether I could. The challenge was exciting in those days; caution came later.

Then there were recitals. Britten and Pears postponed their first *Winterreise* until they were over fifty; I did mine when I was thirty-one. We have known Richard Stangroom (and Nanette) ever since we moved to Sutton; Richard has just retired as conductor of the Banstead Musical Society, after forty-two years. Our recital was to raise funds for the choir. The piece is intense, and almost suicidally self-absorbed; everything the poor man sees (a crow, a signpost) reflects his own grief. I believed in what I was doing, and we worked hard. I learnt two things from the performance: first, that the introduction to *Das Wirthaus*, the twentieth song, though only about a line and a half on the page, is so slow that it gives you time for a breather; and second, that it is only possible to make the last song, *Der Leiermann*, sufficiently cold if you have just sung the other twenty-three songs first. Richard was an excitable pianist in those days, and one or two things which I thought we had decided rather went by the board; but I heard a recording of the first half (before the tape ran out), and it seemed pretty good. I do not know what I would think of it now; it no longer exists.

A few years later, Janet and I did the Schumann opus

39 *Liederkreis* for the same cause, and at the same venue (a barn in Cheam). We worked at this for a whole term, and by the time of the performance we were very comfortable with it – if one can be comfortable with anything so romantically troubled. Accompanying is probably the only context in which Janet does exactly what she is told (though only, she adds, if she trusts the singer).

My best accompanist (I hope it is not unchivalrous to say so) was Frank Martin – not the Swiss composer, but an Englishman, who once caused confusion by performing the *Cinq Preludes* of his namesake. Frank was the husband of an old college friend of Janet's; he was a lovely pianist, and we did a number of recitals together. We did the Schumann *Liederkreis* several times. I have a not very good recording of it; Frank is playing a rather clattery Yamaha, and the microphone was somewhere behind my left shoulder, so the balance is all wrong. But I was impressed, listening to it recently, by the spontaneous-sounding rhythmic fluidity which we got into it; in fact it was carefully rehearsed. Once we did Britten's *Holy Sonnets of John Donne*; the thought terrifies me now, but this was in my self-challenging period. The recording proves that I got through it. Frank also did his own settings of three of my poems, which we did several times.

A year or two ago Frank sent me some excerpts from our recitals, transferred to CD. Some I knew about (the *Liederkreis*, etc.). But some were from a recital I had almost forgotten, and did not know that we had recorded. Subsequently, I remembered having slept poorly the night before, and feeling that I had not done myself justice. One does not go around collecting recordings of oneself, and I had little that I was really pleased with; but five of the Faurés (*Apres un reve, Nell, Claire de lune, Diane Sélenée* and *Prison*) and Gurney's *Sleep*, I would happily play to anyone. I thought and felt through them – brain, body and voice

(I almost wrote 'soul'). There is some slightly gaspy breathing, and more than a smidgeon of self-indulgence (particularly slow tempos). But it is good to have them; they remind me of what I could do.

Around the age of forty, I began to think that solo singing, on top of full time teaching, was rather hard work. It was not that I wanted to stop singing – but it was a different sort of singing I wanted to do. In 1976, Tristram had become a chorister at Winchester Cathedral; the organist was Martin Neary, whom I had known in Cambridge. I mentioned casually in a letter that I would help out if he were short. Back came a reply: would I sing in this concert, these services, and so on. Thus began five rather delightful years.

I had left King's feeling that, for the time being, I had had enough of cathedral music. So much of it was not real music at all (*Nicholson in D flat, Wood in the Phrygian Mode*). I was also still in my longish atheist period; I had been confirmed at school, as we all were, but had drifted away from it. Now, by a rather odd route, but for a musician an entirely logical one, I was drawn back in. God looks after us.

I shall say more about Martin Neary in the next chapter, but he certainly thought big. He would invite the London Symphony Orchestra down, for instance, and conduct them himself. (That the rehearsal was apparently rather fraught is another story.) He put on the Bach Passions in German, with original instruments; everyone does this now, but at the time almost no one did. There were early music concerts (Purcell, Monteverdi) which the BBC regularly broadcast. Peter Pears, aged seventy, sang the Evangelist in the Schutz *Christmas Story* – a little flat, but very expressive. (I was Second Wise Man.)

It was in these years, too, that Martin initiated a series of commissions, particularly from Jonathan Harvey, whose son was a chorister. *The dove descending, I love the Lord, Come Holy Ghost* and the *Magnificat and Nunc Dimittis* were all Winchester commissions; the middle two of these have become standard fare with ambitious cathedrals and chamber choirs. We also sang a lot of John Tavener. Tavener looked like an icon and conducted (occasionally) like a praying mantis. He clearly believed in what he was doing; I never thought, as some of my later Westminster Abbey colleagues did, that he was a mere cynical money-maker. But his music was almost deliberately mindless; it was based on a series of simple formulas, and was ultimately no more than rather boring devotional wallpaper. Martin commissioned a whole series of pieces from him over the years, large and small.

He had a lot of support. The Dean, Michael Stancliffe, was an enthusiast for the arts in all forms; his sermons were small artworks in themselves. The Bishop, John Taylor, produced Harvey's modern oratorio, *Passion and Resurrection*, for television. (Tristram, as an angel, apparently wrecked one take by forgetting to remove his glasses.)

Then there were tours; later, Neary was nicknamed 'Martin of Tours' by a Westminster Abbey precentor. My first was a rather jolly weekend in Paris, but the big one was a three-and-a half-week hike round Canada and the U.S.A.; Tristram and I both went on this. We stayed in hotels, or, more often, private houses. The latter could be a mixed blessing. One does not need, after a day's travelling, a rehearsal and a concert, to have one's host invite the neighbours in, to meet a real live English lay clerk (rhymed with 'berk'). I also remember a particularly ostentatious party in Cincinnati. The guests were all white and the staff all black. A string quartet played in an alcove. "Asparagus and roses," the Bishop murmured; "strange miracles which only money can buy." Both were wildly out of season. "Gee, I don't know how they do it," a guest remarked; "they're not even in the mafia." On the other hand, Tristram and I stayed with a lovely homely couple in Ottawa, where the snow came up to the house-eaves, and it was so cold on the streets one night that you could have died of exposure in half an hour. We had a variety of engagements: evensong for two thousand people in Washington Cathedral, for instance, but also small-town jobs such as a concert in Winchester, Massachusetts; we were celebrating our nine-hundredth anniversary, they their seventy-fifth. Musically, the highlights were Britten's *Hymn to St Cecilia* and Herbert Howells' anthem in memory of John F. Kennedy, *Take him, earth, for cherishing*, which I had not done before. A lower light was being made to sing the verses in the Byrd Four-part Mass in a church in Wall Street, with a serious whisky hangover. From time to time we used a small orchestra (a Mozart mass, Tavener's *Little Requiem*); they were not very good, and Martin sacked them half way round. When the Carnegie Hall organ packed up just before our last concert, they were popularly supposed to have sabotaged it. Afterwards, James Lancelot took me back on stage, and we did the first of the *Liederkreis* songs to an audience of two cleaners. I have sung *lieder* in Carnegie Hall; it would look good on a CV.

I wore out more than one car driving to Winchester; it was a hundred-and-forty-mile round trip. The bigger jobs, though, were quite well paid. The lay clerks made sure that they were; they were always arguing about money. ("How much are we getting for our Channel Islands trip?" "Nothing, gentlemen; you are merely singing your weekend services elsewhere in the diocese." Ha!)

They were a mixed bunch. William Kendall (Willie) was a really fine tenor who perhaps ought to have made more of his career. He was disorganised, a law unto himself, and did not, in those days, always do himself justice. I remember a particularly disappointing *Matthew Passion* in the Festival Hall. But he always (it seemed to me) sang well in Winchester. The other top-class singer was Donald Sweeney, a down-to-earth Geordie with a virile baritone. When we did a Prom one year, he figured on the (alphabetical) Prom soloists' roster between John Shirley-Quirk and Robert Tear – his proper niche, I felt.

At the other end of the scale were Willie's fellow tenors, John Crook and Ken Tewkesbury. (There was no fourth tenor; Martin could never find one good enough.) Both taught in the choir school. John, a rather ordinary singer, eventually inherited some money, and was able to devote himself to photography and architectural research. Ken made a noise like chewed string, but he knew something about singing technique, which he taught to the boys. Tristram as a chorister always knew how to breathe; Jonathan never did, though he was good at snatching breaths in unlikely places. One of the delights of those years was to drive down to evensong and find that Tristram was doing the solo in *Stanford in G*; his voice was clear and utterly safe, but the most expressive phrase was the one where the breathing had him at full stretch.

A further pleasure was to join Keith Ross again; he sang, taught in the choir school, and was in charge of the choristers. On tour in the U.S.A., a rather unstable child threw a huge and tearful tantrum, aimed quite largely at Keith; I wondered what he would do. He let it blow itself out, and then said quietly, "I think I should go and wash your face now."

James Lancelot, yet another Kingsman, was the assistant organist. He was not an exciting musician, but he was meticulous and very reliable. He was a better player than Martin; he once made two small mistakes in a carol service, and we could hardly believe our ears. He had what was almost a speech impediment; one did not always pick up what he was saying. He also walked in a rather strange fashion, due, I think, to a congenital hip problem. He used to play in the annual cricket match against the choristers. If you wanted to pick the worst and most unco-ordinated cricket side in England, you would do well to begin with James and Canon Alex Wedderspoon (later Dean of Guildford). I shall not forget Alex slowly buckling on a pad, and saying in a voice like Eeyore's, "I scored a run once."

In the early 1980s, James's life turned upside down. He met a girl called Sylvia, who sang in a choir he conducted, and for months they wandered around the Close like teenagers who had just discovered holding hands. They married, and soon after, James was appointed to the top job at Durham Cathedral, ahead of several more experienced candidates. According to the rumour-factory, he did a splendid interview; he had a clear vision of what he wanted.

Martin's life failed to turn upside down. When Douglas Guest retired from Westminster Abbey in 1980, Martin was on a shortlist of three, and clearly expected to be appointed. But at the last minute the Abbey authorities persuaded Simon Preston to stand, and gave him the job. Martin could barely hide his disappointment. "Such a pity," said Noel Osborne; "Penny had already measured up for curtains." It was to be another eight years before Martin went to the Abbey.

Winchester, Salisbury and Chichester formed a little coterie; every summer they put on the Southern Cathedrals Festival, which circulated between the three of them. We all knew each other. In 1979, the same year as the Winchester American tour, I went to Normandy as a guest singer with Chichester. It was not a happy trip; at the end of it, the wife of a bass lay clerk ran off with a countertenor. A further problem was planning. It was designed as a part-holiday; there was to be a concert every two days, with the intervening day for beaches, the Bayeux tapestry, or whatever. There was little need to rehearse, as the programme was always the same. But children have to be occupied, and John Birch, the organist, had clearly decided that this was nothing to do with him; he would disappear in his car for a day and a half, and only turn up for the concerts. No one seemed to be in charge. The Dean, an irascible old Kingsman called Holtby, eventually blew his top, to me of all people, in the middle of a street. John Birch left soon after that. He was an odd man; he played Matthew Camidge on a series of rather nice French organs. Cavaillé-Coll was a great admirer of Camidge, Noel told me.

It was during my Winchester years that I began doing Downing Street dinners, with the Martin Neary Singers. Martin had been organist of St Margaret's, Westminster, while Edward Heath was Prime Minister; he fancied himself as a musician, and thought it classy to have entertainment at his official functions. We would sing grace, be wined and dined out of sight somewhere, and perform again later in the evening, a pattern I was used to from King's feasts. I remember a dinner for the Cabinet before the state opening of Parliament, and another for Gough Whitlam, the Australian Prime Minister (*Waltzing Matilda*, of course). It was at the former, I think, that I parked Janet's very old and shabby Ford Thames van at the far end of Downing Street, and later, well over the drink-drive limit, had to reverse it past rows of ministerial Rolls-Royces, guided by several policemen. Once we went to Chequers; Edward Heath came to the rehearsal, and made comments. ("Can you hear the words?" "Oh, are there any?") But the most extraordinary was the William Walton seventieth birthday dinner. Bliss and Howells wrote pieces for this, and came to our rehearsal; both were over eighty. Bliss's piece was rather boring, but the Howells grace was lovely. The words were by Robert Armstrong, the civil servant who was later to be rather famously 'economical with the truth'. I sang the solo in Walton's *Set me as a seal*, to the entire musical establishment of England – Britten, Solti, Menuhin, Walton himself, and so on. The London Sinfonietta did bits of *Façade*, and at midnight, John Lill and two others played the Schubert B flat Trio. We were to mingle with the guests – but how does one mingle with such people? (The Queen Mother, Lord Harewood...) One of our sopranos had her bottom pinched by Malcolm Arnold; it was the best we could do.

I shall also mention here, though it happened later, the premiere of Andrew Lloyd Webber's *Requiem* in New York; we had previously recorded it in England. It is a help for a composer to be rich. A prototype of the *Requiem* had been done at Lloyd Webber's little festival at Sydmonton, but later he paid for a try-out of the full version, with choir, soloists and orchestra, in a BBC studio; there was a baritone soloist in this version, I remember, who disappeared later. Lloyd Webber had a small music staff of his own: an orchestration wizard, and two cut-and-paste men who made alterations in the score and parts up to the last minute, and even between the sessions. The piece itself was in a mixture of styles, with a particularly saccharine *Pie Jesu*, which eventually reached single figures in the pop charts – the only time I have appeared there. The soloists were Sarah Brightman, Placido Domingo and Piers Miles-Kingston, the Winchester head chorister. Sarah Brightman, the then Mrs. Lloyd Webber, had a small voice of extraordinary range, which her husband exploited. Placido's voice is huge; one does not completely realise this until one is in the same studio. There was a rhythm in the *Benedictus* which never went quite right; "Perhaps they don't have syncopation in opera," James suggested.

Placido and I share a taste for bread and butter pudding, a fact which I discovered in the Abbey Road canteen. As to Piers Miles-Kingston, I chiefly remember his mother – in wonderful furs.

Lorin Maazel, who conducted, looked like a large frog. He had an amazing memory: "Bar three hundred and eighty-two," he would say, with no reference to the score. The premiere was in St Thomas's, New York; subsequently, we did it in Westminster Abbey, and the Vienna Musikverein. We were lucky in Vienna. We were supposed to fly in late on a Saturday, and leave early the following morning. But there was snow, and our flight was delayed, so we had several hours to explore Vienna – a magical place, to which I would return every year if I could.

The Lloyd Webber experience marked a brief return to Winchester, after a period away. In 1981, Tristram left the cathedral choir; they had also by this time acquired a regular fourth tenor, so there was less for me to do. But I wanted to do more; here was an environment in which I felt comfortable.

My original contact with Guildford Cathedral was a happy accident. I had begun composing again, and my publisher (Barry Brunton) told me that Guildford had bought copies of my men's voice *Magnificat and Nunc Dimittis*. So I went to hear it. I immediately took to Philip Moore, the organist, and I also discovered that they were short of tenors – down to one regular, in fact. I began filling in when I could, and soon offered to do the job full-time. There was no audition, and two weeks later I was appointed. I still had Winchester commitments, but after two terms' heavy deputising, I started properly in September, 1981.

Guildford was different. To begin with, there were no arguments about money because everybody knew that there was none. We were paid, of course, but it was a fifty-mile round trip (a hundred on Sundays), and the salary did little more than cover my petrol. Early in my time, I remember piling into cars after evensong to do a recital at the wrong end of the diocese; I got home about midnight. There was no fee. The Winchester men would never have stood for it.

Though a new cathedral – it had only been going for twenty years – it had more traditions than anywhere I had ever known. The whole history of the place was contained in people's memories, particularly the comic history, and it was kept fresh by constant re-telling. The old-timers revered Barry Rose, who had started the choir from scratch. He had huge energy and commitment, and though his conducting was unconventional ("The beat is irrelevant"), he could get musical results from almost anyone. His only qualification was ARCO (failed).

Philip succeeded Barry. He was delightful. He was probably too nice to be a top-class choir trainer (though there were occasional tempers), but a sort of musicality always came through. He was a composer; we sang a lot of his music, and he was generous to fellow-workers. He was also a Duruflé fan; we seemed to do the *Requiem* endlessly – a wonderful piece. On tour in France, we did a concert of *Messiah* excerpts; only Philip could have done Duruflé's *Ubi caritas* as an encore.

Every choir seems to have one member who is allowed to sing louder than the others, and one funny old boy. At Winchester, these were, respectively, William Kendall and John Davies, an eccentric schoolmaster who, among other things, never seemed to wash. Guildford's funny old boy was John Burrows-Watson (JBW). He had a speaking voice like a BBC announcer, and a laugh (much imitated) which resembled a series of 'Hear, hears!' in the House of Lords. Exactly ten years older than I, he seemed to have done a number of jobs (National Trust caretaker, school bursar, gentleman's gentleman, an employment agency), none of which lasted very long. He had white hair, and not much of it; when I last saw him, he had dyed it a tawny brown.

The loud singer was Simon Deller, son of the famous Alfred. I am told that he was a slow developer, but by the time I knew him, he was a fine baritone with a large range. He was not only loud but early, because he insisted on singing dead on the beat regardless of what the rest of us did. He was a man of firm views. Once a year we had to do a modern form of liturgy for the Bishop – 'And also with you', that sort of thing. Simon would have none of it. Arms folded across his chest, "And with thy Spirit," he would pray, as loudly as possible. ("Would you say you were a flexible man, Simon?" I once asked him.) His view of any new piece was that if he could not get it right second time, then it was obviously rubbish; he was not a great sight-reader. He was Deputy Head of Lanesborough School, later becoming Head; Lanesborough provided the boys, though it was never an official choir school.

There were other good singers. Pip Newton (alto) eventually went on to St Paul's, as did Mervyn Collins (tenor). Adrian Peacock, an arrogant young bass choral scholar, went to Westminster Cathedral. Then there was Michael Barry, known as 'Self', a good alto in those days, and a real enthusiast; he used to travel forty miles from Hayward's Heath on a moped. For a while he stood next to Chris Trueblood, an American, who sang well when he was sober; but he had visa trouble, and lasted only a year.

David Gibbs was a fairly ordinary singer, as he would be the first to admit. "Am I programmed for this?" he would say, peering suspiciously at an unfamiliar piece. He had sung at the opening service in 1961, and was still going in occasionally forty years later. He was intelligent, an English graduate with an apt line in quotation. I remember Simon leading the choristers across a pedestrian crossing in Rouen – a large and commanding presence. "And all the trumpets sounded for him on the other side," said David. He once told me about his evacuation during the war; his parents had put him on a train and said that they would see him at the weekend. They did not meet for four years. "I resolved never to trust anybody ever again," he told me. He married Elizabeth, but not until he was nearly forty, which perhaps had something to do with it.

My first Guildford tour was an eye-opener. With Winchester, I had stayed in hotels or (sometimes rather grand) private houses; for Guildford it was a youth hostel. It had dormitories for eight or so, some of them unisex; one contained (among others) Simon and Mollie Deller, Philip, and a German coach driver (Mollie pinched his nose to stop him snoring). One night a cat ran over me as I slept. We sang in St Maclou in Rouen; it has a wonderful acoustic. (Guildford is terrible: dead as a doornail. It was built for the spoken word.) I have a recording of the Duruflé *Requiem* from St Maclou; it still sounds rather good. We also did other venues – Beauvais Cathedral, for instance, where I sang *Messiah* solos. On the last night we dined in the square where Joan of Arc was burnt.

The Dean in those days was Tony Bridge, a large man in every sense, with a voice redolent of brandy and cigars. He delighted in telling congregations that he had been an atheist till the age of forty. (I saw the light a little earlier.) He was not noted for his tact. He used to swear in sermons – "Bloody hell!" And he once greeted a MENCAP congregation on a hot afternoon with "You must be MAD to come in here on a day like this!" But he was a great choir supporter. One year the cathedral deficit exactly equalled the cost of the music; to an accountant, there is an obvious answer. "We can't do without the music," said Tony. "What would we have here? Just four old clerics stuck on a hill." This was particularly enlightened as the average weekday congregation was (perhaps) four; sometimes we sang to nobody. He was in marked contrast to Canon Peter Croft. One day we did the Tallis *Lamentations, part ii*. "Isn't there a shorter version of *The Lamentations*?" he asked. Someone took him aside and put him right.

Philip moved to York Minster in 1982, and was succeeded by Andrew Millington. This caused some unhappiness. It was the classic situation where those within the community want the deputy to be moved up, which in fact rarely happens. The deputy was Peter Wright, who was a good player, and knew what he wanted from the choir. He was also deeply committed to the place, and we liked him. The appointing panel was widely representative, but contained only one musician, Sebastian Forbes, Professor at Surrey University, which was just down the hill. Philip sat in on the interviews, but had no vote. The panel went for Andrew, largely on account of his superior-looking CV. "Peter has less on his CV because he has devoted himself to the cathedral," said Philip. Peter was upset. In 1989 he moved to Southwark, where he has been happily in charge ever since.

Meanwhile, Andrew took over in his straightforward fashion, and we all settled down. But I was feeling a little weary by this time; I needed a rest. In fact I resigned twice; first I said I would just do Sundays and Mondays, then I gave up even that. (Later, I did a year of men-only Mondays, as they seemed to be short; there were a number of these part-time arrangements.) I remember being quite desperately upset after my last Guildford Christmas; I thought I was saying goodbye to this sort of thing for ever. Fortunately, I was wrong.

It has been good to catch up with Andrew and Madeleine in his new post at Exeter. Madeleine, an artist who works in textiles, does not sit on the fence. "How was the girls' evensong?" she asked. "Nice and gentle." "Just what I tell Andrew: no balls!"

I enjoyed the Guildford years; the Winchester-Guildford era was probably my best as a singer. I was gradually giving up my solo work, but I still felt in touch with it. Things that I had previously found tricky – the little solo in *Harwood in A flat*, for instance – no longer held any terrors. Neither did being the first of only two tenors in the *Missa Papae Marcelli*, or E.W.Naylor's *Vox Dicentis*. Eight services a week on top of full-time teaching taxed the voice a little, but mostly one coped. I remember a ridiculous day when I taught all eight periods, drove to Guildford, rehearsed, and recorded a BBC broadcast evensong, at the end of which I sang the verses in the Advent Prose ('Drop down, ye heavens, from above'); I still have this on tape. I loved doing plainsong, particularly being cantor in the psalms; more than once I did alternate verses of the whole of Psalm 78. The trick was, I thought, to be just expressive enough with the words, but no more.

I thought I would do nothing for a bit, but this did not last; within a couple of months, I had applied for a job at The Royal Hospital, Chelsea. The Royal Hospital ran a professional choir of twelve adults: five sopranos, contralto, counter-tenor, two tenors and three basses. The Hospital itself was a Wren building, or series of buildings, founded in Charles II's time; his influence was still felt. The Hospital possessed more than one Van Dyck portrait, and the Collect for the Royal Hospital began: 'O God, who by the overshadowing of an oak didst preserve our Royal Founder from the hands of his enemies…', commemorating his escape after the Battle of Worcester. The pensioners, on formal occasions or when outside the Hospital, still wore the original red coats, and lived in the rather small wooden cubicles. The qualifications for entry were to be in receipt of an army pension (long service or disability) and to have no dependants. An unwritten qualification was to be non-commissioned. Apart from the adjutant, the staff were all retired officers.

The first Governor I was aware of was General Sir Richard Ford, a nice old buffer who read the lesson as though he were telling a kids' story on *Jackanory*. He was succeeded by General Sir Roland Guy, who was more intelligent. When he arrived, he told me, he set himself to learn all the pensioners' names (close on three hundred of them) from photographs, at the rate of five a day. He also said that a two-minute walk from one building to another might take as much as three-quarters of an hour, because old soldiers would want to show him crumpled press cuttings, or tell him their life story. He realised that this was important, and allowed himself the time.

The choir was one of the friendliest I have ever joined. I forget how soon it was that Annie embraced me, but probably after about three weeks. Annie and Mike, a small and jovial alto who sometimes deputised, had a rather semi-detached marriage; they each had outside interests. There was, apparently, more of this sort of thing going on than I realised. One lovely, bubbly soprano, who did *Stanford in G* most movingly on our trip to York, had a complicated love life. She had a brief fling with a counter-tenor, but tried to run him in tandem with someone else, to which he did not take kindly. I wrote a piece for her second wedding, a rather over-the-top affair which concluded with the Tallis forty-part motet, the bride and groom singing in choir five. The marriage lasted two years. (I remember Mike and I watching her lean over in a low-cut dress to rub something out in her copy; things wobbled, rather delightfully. "She really oughtn't to do that," said Mike.)

A third soprano was clearly having an affair with yet another colleague, while her husband consoled himself elsewhere. Eventually he decided to study for the priesthood. "You can't be a priest," I told him; "you tell such terrible jokes." ("Who's Googie Withers?" "Anyone's does in this cold weather.") But he was ordained, and got a cathedral job – from which he was sacked for having an affair. This made the tabloids.

The regular Sunday service was shortened Choral Matins; the army is a low-church institution. Compared with a cathedral, we sang rather little: an introit in the octagon (a sort of ante-chapel, with the only decent acoustic in the place), the first set of Responses, a congregational canticle and psalm, some hymns, an anthem and a final Amen, which was always preceded by the National Anthem. Remembrance Sunday was a big event; there were also weddings, memorials, two annual concerts, seasonal extras at Christmas and Easter, and the odd trip elsewhere, such as our week in York Minster – about the jolliest choir tour I have ever been on.

The director of music was Ian Curror. The statutes state that the organist should be the deserving daughter of an army officer; but the Hospital finally decided that they wanted a real musician, and appointed Ian. I knew from the start that I would like him. He was well-organised, and he looked after people. The copies were meticulously marked, and he knew what he wanted: "The *crescendo* starts on the third beat, not the second." However, though he clearly had a soul, I occasionally wondered whether quite all of it got into the music-making. He did not get on with Denys Bartlett, the crusty old Welsh chaplain, who thought that choirs should sing for love, not money. (Not as extreme a view as that held by Alan Luff, Precentor of Westminster Abbey; he was overheard to say that choirs were idolatrous.)

Because there was so little service music, we rehearsed it very thoroughly. Concerts, though, were rather a rush

– perhaps because rehearsals cost money. The first I did consisted of the Allegri *Miserere*, the Byrd Four-part Mass (complete), and *Jesu, meine Freude*; we sang all this without a break. There was only one other tenor, and the fee was (perhaps) £15. I felt it was well earned.

On our free day during the York week, some of us went to Fountains Abbey, and there we cooked up a scheme for singing all our favourite eight-part music, one to a part. Thus was born the Fountains Consort, which I directed. We did an evensong in Winchester Cathedral, and several concerts. The trouble with one's favourite eight-part music is that much of it is rather slow. We began the first concert with Gibbons' *O clap your hands* (quite lively), but after that it was Purcell's *Hear my prayer*, *Faire is the heaven*, Pearsall's *Lay a garland* – and so on. We also did the Allegri *Miserere*. At a later concert, we started with Bach's *Der Geist Hilft*; we sang it at written pitch, and it soon went a semitone sharp, which was rather terrifying. In the second half we did the first one-to-a-part performance of my *Mater Dei*.

It was about this time that I heard Charles Brett's madrigal group, the Amaryllis Consort. They were never entirely successful, I thought, partly because you need light voices for this sort of thing, and he had too many big singers: Stephen Roberts, Michael George. Another difficulty was one I was discovering for myself: directing from the middle, you can control ensemble, but you cannot really hear balance or blend. Though it was fun, therefore, it would in the end have become unsatisfying.

Chelsea was an interlude, and one which I greatly enjoyed. Now my life was to take a new turn.

Nine

SINGING (II)

LATE IN 1989, casting around for a way out of teaching, I came across a two-day-a-week job as librarian at the Royal College of Organists. I was quite unqualified for this, and it only paid a pittance, but Janet reminded me that the RCO President was Martin Neary, so I rang him up. To my surprise, he suggested that I apply to Westminster Abbey as a Lay Vicar. My first reaction was that I was forty-eight and not likely to get any better; but realising that I was talking myself out of a job, I changed tack, and in due course was auditioned and appointed. Thus began some of the best years of my life, and at the same time some of the oddest.

My appointment itself was odd enough. Why should Neary have wanted someone of my age, who had never been a full-time professional? The answer has to be his quite dreadful start at the Abbey after his appointment in 1988. I was not there at the beginning, but by the time of my arrival the main incidents were already part of the mythology. The choir petitioned the Dean and Chapter about Neary's incompetence; of course the Chapter had to back their own appointment. Neary and the Precentor decided not to renew one of the Lay Vicars' five-year contracts, on the grounds (Neary's words to me) that they 'wanted a change'. The Lay Vicar pointed out that when the new contracts were introduced, Simon Preston, the previous organist, had said that the only reason for non-renewal would be vocal decline, and on Simon's confirming this he had to be re-instated. There were verbal and written warnings, and suspensions. One Lay Vicar was suspended a) for putting an added sixth into the last chord of a broadcast carol (known subsequently as a Westminster sixth), and b) for referring to Neary, in front of the choristers, as 'fart-face'. A disciplinary hearing exonerated him on both counts. His defence to the first charge was that he so entirely failed to understand Neary's beat that he did not know when the last chord had begun. The questioning of a witness went somewhat as follows:

> Q Were you surprised when Mr. X was suspended?
> A: No.
> Q: Why not?
> A: Because the atmosphere was so poisonous that something was bound to happen.

And so on.

Neary appointed me, then, because I was outside the London professional scene, and because I had worked contentedly enough for him in the past. This was, I think, implicit between us, but it was made clearer by others. Ian Curror told me that when the Abbey asked him for a reference, the questions were mainly about loyalty and co-operation, rather than musical ability. And the Dean, Michael Mayne, in an interview before I started, wanted to establish that I was willing to work with Neary (as others, apparently, were not), and also pointed out that, as a known associate of his, I might have a sticky start.

In fact it was not particularly sticky. I kept rather quiet, and felt my way. The suspicion that I must be Neary's spy, which itself shows how far the poison had spread, died a natural death. Two colleagues, later to become good friends, were rather cool at first, but everyone else was amiable enough. John Buttrey, the senior Lay Vicar, went out of his way to be kind and helpful, for which I have always been grateful.

But it was not only the musical atmosphere which was strained; the community as a whole, in spite of talk from the pulpit of the 'Abbey family', did not seem to me an entirely happy one. It was the sort of place where different groups peered suspiciously at each other, where non-musicians would pretend not to know one for at least a year, and then suddenly start using one's Christian name. The Precentor, Alan Luff, in charge of choir welfare, did not speak to me for almost twelve months. In fact, the only thing which seemed to unite a singularly disunited community was that everyone disliked ... well, never mind. (Not, in fact, Martin Neary.)

That relations between the choir and the Dean and Chapter were rather cool could be explained by the events of the previous two years. But in fact the Abbey's musical history has always been somewhat fractious. Sir Ernest Bullock had left in a huff, and so (more or less) had Simon Preston. One can read about plenty of ructions between the Dean and Chapter and the musicians in Trevor Beeson's *Window on Westminster (A Canon's Diary, 1976-87)*. And the musicians have not always got on with each other. One of my colleagues had been suspended for pushing another into a cupboard. Simon Preston did little for human relations when he told the Lay Vicars, a year after his arrival, that most of them had been there long enough, and that they ought to consider their positions. (Contractually, he could do nothing about it, and they stayed.) Rodney Williams once described to me all the musical rows at the Abbey back to the time of Turle. This sort of thing is self-perpetuating.

None of it bothered me particularly. My colleagues (in due course my friends) were the other singers. Asked how I was getting on, "Oh," said Janet, "they're a crowd of eccentrics; he fits in very well." "*This* is the Abbey family," said one of them, waving his arms bibulously and benignly round a choir gathering. Besides, I was singing without having to teach; I felt as though I was on holiday.

The two who had treated me coolly at first, Chris Tipping and Andrew Giles, were (it is fair to say) violently anti-Neary. Aside from more general reasons, this was partly because they had been buddies of Simon Preston, and had lost their power-base, and partly because they both had what seemed to me a considerable build-up of internal anger for reasons quite unconnected with the Abbey. Chris was trying to do something rather difficult: as well as the Abbey choir, he was a partner in a nearby law firm, work which he described to me as 'a mixture of stress and boredom'. He was also, and out of a genuine desire to help, our choir representative; he negotiated on our behalf with Neary and the Dean and Chapter over pay, conditions of service, contracts, disciplinary matters, and so on. He would regularly arrive just in time for a practice, looking harassed, and be met by somebody with a problem. His family were clearly difficult; he had trained as a musician against his parents' wishes, for instance. He had also had a disastrous first marriage. His salvation, I thought, was his second wife, Sally.

Andrew's background was similarly uneasy, and his first marriage had also broken up. During my time at the Abbey he married a Japanese girl half his age; it lasted two years. He had been a promising counter-tenor, but had lost it; the bottom of the voice was still there, but the top was in shreds, and of course he was aware of this. One usually knew how he felt; on bad days, he would announce his arrival by kicking the door down. He was difficult, but after an uneasy start I found I liked him: quick, warm, intelligent, witty – the one-liners go by so fast that if you blink you miss them – and (once) a friend in need. He has settled down again with a lady called Alison; we think it will work.

The other altos were Mike Lees, younger and more normal than most, with a wife and two small children, and Simon Gay – Glad – who had a high, almost female-sounding voice, and was, he told me, the Abbey's first openly gay Lay Vicar. We were all Equity members except Glad, who was Musicians' Union – the soloists' union; Equity was for chorus singers. Like many queers, he was a hot source of gossip. "Oh, that's public knowledge now, is it?" he would say, when one had offered him a particularly juicy tit-bit. His heart was in the right place. Andrew teased him unmercifully.

I began singing next to John New. John had an unremarkable voice, which he managed with some skill. He never showed much enthusiasm. He had, I think, a number of talents which he mostly kept rather well hidden, though he did organise (very efficiently) our luggage for choir tours – forty pieces, perhaps, which had to be negotiated round a series of airports, trains, coaches, and so on. James Wilkinson's book, *Westminster Abbey: A Thousand Years of Music and Pageant* (2003), tells of a singing man who, starting as a boy chorister soon after the Reformation, survived a wide variety of doctrines and liturgies (Henry VIII, Edward VI, Mary, Elizabeth…), before finally retiring in 1596. This, I thought, was John. "Well,"

I can hear him say, "they kept on changing things, but I just sang the notes."

The tenors on the other side were John Buttrey and John Nixon. I had first known John Buttrey in Cambridge as a John's choral scholar, though he was ten years older than I; he was Australian, and had come up the hard way. He had wanted to be an academic, but this had not worked out, so he made a career out of singing, while continuing to write the book on seventeenth-century theatre which has occupied much of his life. He had had eight years with the Deller Consort, but fell out with Alfred. At one time he was close to Chris, but they fell out, too. Perhaps he was not very flexible, and he was certainly against all change. I once asked him if he could think of a single change at the Abbey which he *had* approved of; after much thought, he came up with one he had suggested himself.

John was forcibly retired eighteen months after my arrival; he did not want to go, and took the Abbey to an industrial tribunal. He argued, firstly, that although our contract stipulated a retiring age of sixty, other Abbey workers could go on until sixty-five, and secondly, that when the contracts were introduced, it was understood that anyone still fit to sing could continue to do so – as had, indeed, sometimes happened. He lost his case; the written contract takes precedence over the verbal. There was a certain amount of dirty linen, which the press enjoyed, and John was for a while *persona non grata* at the Abbey. But he partly proved his point by deputising at St Paul's for another five years.

John Nixon is at the same time one of the most warm-hearted people I know, and one of the more irritating to sing by. There was an element of the keen prep school boy about him; he was constantly volunteering for things, or pointing out what he thought we might have missed. He usually sang a little too loudly, and slightly ahead of the beat – his early leads were famous – as though the rest of us could not cope unless he led. He was also twitchy and excitable; no music went by without his comment – often while we were singing it. Every nine months or so I would become seriously irritated, and he would know that I was. But he never let the sun go down upon my wrath; before the evening was out, he would ring up, and we would put things right. He was an early music singer; Gothic Voices was his group. Once he sang a little Mendelssohn solo on an Abbey broadcast. "You did a passable imitation of a romantic tenor," I told him. "Do you enjoy this sort of thing?" "I despise it," he said.

Of the basses, I began by standing next to Simon Birchall. Simon took a rather semi-detached view of the Abbey; he did a lot of outside work. He was very tall and very quiet; he hardly said a word, though you could get him to open up, I found, if you asked about his children. He had a fine voice with a huge range; I once heard him sing the top F sharp in the last chorus of Wesley's *Ascribe unto the Lord*, and the optional bottom B at the end of Howells' *Take him, earth, for cherishing*, in the same rehearsal. As a concert soloist, he was not outgoing enough; he was a singer, not a performer.

Lawrence Wallington *was* a performer; he sang Byrd as though it was opera. But he had not quite got Simon's voice. Like John Buttrey, he could be pernickety, and once a month he would throw a wobbly. Once he tore up a lot of photocopies Neary had done, on the grounds that copying music was illegal; unfortunately, these were authorised by the publisher. He could also be rather pompous. Returning from a spell with the Monteverdis, he was struck by some minor omission (of mine, I think). "Things are getting very slack in this choir," he said. I used to pull his leg; after he had worked out that it was nonthreatening, he quite liked it. Most of the time he was fun, though you never knew what line he would take next.

Lawrence sang next to Roger Cleverdon. Roger potentially had a fine, noble baritone, but he suffered from nerves. He would launch two or three magnificent solo phrases – the opening of Vaughan Williams' *Rise, heart*, for instance – and then sing a perfectly ordinary one flat. One Sunday morning he leant across during the second lesson. "Singing is a most unnatural business," he said. I knew what he meant. He was a dear.

Finally, there was Rodney Williams. They do not come more eccentric than Rodney. His interests were limited but intense, being confined almost entirely to glees, cider, Victorian church music, 78 rpm records of singers (English, no opera) – and attractive young men. He lived with his mother in Bromley, in a house stuck in the 1930s, with a black and white TV. He conducted a local choral society, mostly rather old, who put on things like Barnby's *Daughter of Jairus*. He liked the old; he revered the old lay vicars who were at the Abbey when he began, and often talked about them. (I remember rather unwisely mentioning a name at coffee-time; it provoked a lengthy monologue. "Now look what you've done," said Glad.) Another hero was Boris Ord, for whom he had sung as a treble at King's. His stories usually ended, "He's dead, you know."

He had a huge fount of knowledge and reference, into which I sometimes tapped. "What chant would have been sung to the *Nunc Dimittis* at Thomas Hardy's Abbey funeral?" – that sort of thing. He once, to the surprise of his colleagues, wrote a very erudite review of a glee collection for *The Musical Times*, and quite recently he has been lecturing on Charles Wood in the States. But mostly he did not do anything with his knowledge; he just liked to know things. He once told me about a Battishill manuscript he bought at auction; the British Museum wanted it, but he got there first. He would persuade Neary and young Martin Baker to re-introduce duff pieces by old Abbey organists: *Cooke in G, Arnold in A.* He astonished a visiting deputy by announcing that "Attwood was a better composer than Mozart." And when challenged: "Mozart wasn't English." I once wrote him a rude glee – words and music: it is apparently very popular with the Noblemen's and Gentlemen's Catch Club, which meets in the House of Lords. I have never heard it.

As to the young men, he was quite blatant. "Were *you* in the navy?" asked an innocent female, after a comment about his descending a ladder, naval-fashion. "No," he replied, "I just like sailors." "He seems a nice young man," he would say, of some new deputy. And he enjoyed watching tennis, about which he knew nothing – but there were those nice young men in shorts; Tim Henman was a particular favourite. John New once persuaded him that there was a Tim Henman calendar, and he had several newsagents in Bromley looking out for it. Even he did not quite believe that it was a pop-up calendar.

A lot of my colleagues thought he was a fool, and in some ways he was; he played up to his foolish image. He could also be a bore. But there was no one like him.

All of this, of course, I took in gradually; to begin with, I had concerns of my own. I was starting a new career at the age of forty-eight, with a drop in salary and some financial risk. (I had to pass a probationary year; my contract came up for renewal after five.) Though never a really high tenor, I was on Decani – the high tenor side. I was not always in good vocal health. (Later, I had my tonsils out, which helped, as did a move to Cantoris.) I had to prove myself. It was all rather public.

Yet at the same time, it was impossible not to be aware

of the atmosphere around me; this was something new. The London singing scene is fairly hard-nosed; provincial cathedrals, by and large, are gentler. Of course one knew that professionals could give conductors a hard time, but I had never experienced it myself. Was Neary, musically and personally, really as bad as they all made out? And if so, why had I not minded working for him before? The answer to the latter, I discovered, lay in the difference between the two situations. My singing at Winchester was not really work at all; it was a rather delightful hobby, the jam on the bread. Though the Winchester lay clerks moaned about Neary from time to time, I did not feel inclined to join them; it was good to be singing with Tristram, and I was glad to be asked. Besides, I was only a deputy; I was not there every day. Now, suddenly, the Abbey services (and the rest) *were* the bread; this was my work, and my relationship with Neary was, among other things, a professional one. I judged him as I would previously have judged a headmaster. As to my colleagues, they took time off to sing for John Eliot Gardiner, Harry Christophers, and so on, and made comparisons, as they did (quite naturally) with Simon Preston.

And gradually I came to see that, allowing for a little exaggeration, they were more or less right, and it was not only I who felt that, over the years, Neary was actually getting worse. It is invidious to write about the faults in someone's work; we all have faults. Yet without giving at least an indication, it is hard to explain or justify what went on. And faults, alas, there were.

He seemed, for a start, unable to find a naturally singable tempo, the sort of tempo that sings itself. Usually, he was too slow; occasionally (Purcell's *Hear my prayer*) too fast. Partly this was because he had no sense of dance; even if the tempo was right, there were hold-ups at the end of every phrase.

Often he had difficulty establishing a tempo at all. His introductory upbeat, when discernible, did not always relate to what came next. Sometimes he would start a piece quite briskly, immediately decide it was too fast, and try to slow it down. Or the boys would come in slower than he indicated, and he followed them. Or the men, sometimes in collusion with the organist, would set their own tempo, and he followed us. (I remember a hilarious *Zadok* in Oslo; would he be cross, or would he pretend he meant it?)

He appeared only to conduct the top line; there were great holes in the music where the boys had to breathe, while the rest of us were left to fend for ourselves.

His beat itself was grotesque; the second beat in 3/4, for instance, was always absurdly early. Sometimes we amused ourselves by singing what he actually beat; at others, we ignored him.

In any case, he did not really hear; he was reputedly deaf in one ear. All sorts of errors went by unremarked, particularly on Cantoris, the deaf-ear side.

Then there was his Psalm-accompaniment in the Song School; we would hear him rehearsing the boys, bashing out a thick piano chord on every syllable. Of course they sang with no line or sense of phrasing.

And so on. As to his personality, the most prominent feature was a hugely-inflated idea of his own importance. Orchestras picked this up very quickly. One Christmas he was rehearsing (I think) the English Chamber Orchestra when there was a big football match on. At a convenient break, he asked, "Does anyone know the score?" "*Messiah*?" suggested Neil Black, the oboe player. "No, the football score." "Oh, I thought it was a rare moment of self-doubt." This was almost the only time I saw him blush with embarrassment; usually, he did not notice the effect he had on people. It did not help that he had a limited sense of humour, though he was quite good at laughing in what he took to be the right places.

And then he did not treat us all the same. He was wary of those choirmen with whom he had had run-ins, and consulted them about everything ("What do you think, John?"); others of us could safely be ignored. I once pointed this out, but it made little difference.

Fortunately, the twelve of us all got on (more or less), partly because we were united in a sort of common discontent. There was a whole series of catch-phrases – Old Abbey Jokes – based mostly on things which Neary had said or done. They would not look very funny written down, but they were a way in which we communicated. There was no hierarchy; though we were of widely different ages – the range when I left was twenty-three to fifty-eight – we were all on a level. I was just as likely to have my leg pulled by the young as by (for instance) Andrew, who pulled everyone's leg all the time. I liked this; it was fun.

It is remarkable, in retrospect, how much of our life consisted of *not* working with Neary, working against the grain. People would stagger out of the long Friday practices insisting it was the worst rehearsal they had ever been to. Charlie Pott, who sometimes deputised, would become apoplectic. I told him to stay away in the end; it was bad for his blood pressure.

But Neary was not the whole story; as I have indicated, we were an embattled group. We were not very popular with the Dean and Chapter, partly because of my colleagues' petition, partly because Lay Vicars never had been. (And there was a social element: though some of us wore the same academic hood as the Dean, we were still seen as rather below the salt.) One Canon apparently thought that the answer was to sack all the Lay Vicars and start again. I have also mentioned the Precentor, Alan Luff; though head of the choral foundation, he rarely spoke to us, and we were never invited to his house. It was a relief when he left for Birmingham Cathedral.

❖

This, then, was our working atmosphere. We were contracted for eight services a week: three on Sundays, and five weekday evensongs. But there were also concerts (in the Abbey and elsewhere), recordings (none of them very good), tours, and a whole series of Special Services.

I have mentioned Neary and tours before. During my time, we did two three-week trips to the USA, a fortnight in Hungary and Switzerland, and shorter visits to Berlin (twice), Halle, Moscow, Kiev, Oslo, Cologne, and the South of France. On the first Berlin trip we also did a concert in St Thomas, Leipzig – Bach's church; I have sung *Der Geist Hilft* just a couple of feet from where the old boy is buried.

On our first American tour, I kept a journal:

> 20/9/92
> …Glad, who knows everything, explains that the way to get through U.S. customs is to act profoundly English. As he is wearing his *commedia del' arte* shirt at the time, topped with Mexican bandit sunglasses, I suggest that theory outruns practice in this instance. "I do the voice jolly well," he says.

> 21/9
> …Roger (with whom I share a room) is interrupted by our chambermaid this morning in a state of total nudity. She gives him her "I've seen it all before" look, and indeed seems remarkably unimpressed.

27/9
...Rehearsal in the Lutheran Church, Minneapolis. Glad sings the violin tune in the *Hymn to Saint Cecilia*. "I didn't know open strings could do vibrato," says Andrew.

29/9
...in Minneapolis we premiere a commissioned piece by one Eric Hemberg (whom Neary announces as Homburg). I have a small mishap, round about top A – after which Nixon and I contribute little but snorts and giggles. This was naughty, I suppose – but it was not a good piece.

10/10
...Chris thinks he has found a book called *The Rapist's Guide to Sexual Satisfaction*, but the first two words are really one.

And so on. I enjoyed tours; they were a bonding exercise. The travel was interesting, and though our hosts were a varied lot, we met some good people. In Berlin, I stayed with a pair of married doctors; Thomas is a neurosurgeon. Later, I found that he was a Shakespeare fan; standing on a pavement, we recited together the whole of 'Let me not to the marriage of true minds'. I wondered how many English surgeons quote Goethe.

Special services could be regular or occasional: the annual Florence Nightingale service, or Princess Diana's funeral. The Florence Nightingale was always awaited eagerly by the younger element; they had visions, usually disappointed, of an Abbey full of gorgeous young nurses. Another regular was the Battle of Britain service, with the

RAF band in the organ loft, and the Roll of Honour borne to the altar to a Walton march (*Richard III*, usually). Then there was the Judges' service: the legal establishment of England, wigged and gowned, milling around at their ease in the empty nave. They took a long time to seat themselves, and sang the hymns as though back in their Public School chapels. Then they processed off to the Houses of Parliament through Poets' Corner. One year, Martin Baker played them my *Veni Creator* variations as they went. Rather different was the Children of Courage service. The awards were always broadly similar: variations on the boy who had had seventeen operations but was still smiling, and the girl who had rescued her mother from drowning. It was a weepie. One year the certificates were presented by Fergie, who – unforgivably, with a nave full of children – arrived late. She also brought her own children, who misbehaved.

The most memorable one-offs were the memorial services. Soon after I arrived, we did Eva Turner's. Geraint Evans read from a Mozart letter, Gwyneth Jones sang 'Elizabeth's Greeting' from *Tanhauser*, and towards the end there was the voice of Dame Eva herself in *'In questa reggia'* from *Turandot*, a recording I had loved for thirty years.

Eight months later came Sir Geraint's own memorial. The cast was even more starry: Solti, Haitink, Colin Davis and Edward Downes, the Covent Garden chorus and orchestra. Bryn Terfel sang 'Lord God of Abraham', from *Elijah*, the first two-and-a-bit phrases, unbelievably, in one breath; later came the big monologue from *Falstaff*. Thomas Allen did *Figaro*, Dame Gwyneth sang 'Elizabeth's Greeting' again, there were excerpts from *Die Meistersinger*. But the bit which almost finished me off (it only happened twice in the Abbey) was the trio from *Cosi*: Amanda Roocroft, Anne Howells, Stafford Dean. We sang very little ourselves; it was good just to be there.

Years later, we did Solti's own memorial service. My main memories are of a slightly comic rehearsal. Towards the end, all the performers moved to the Sanctuary steps for the final chorus of the *St John Passion*. Gwynne Howell, very Welsh, placed himself between Roger and Lawrence. "I've been told to stand here," he said, "because I can't sight-read." Then we had to make our way back to our places. Neary's attempt to explain this was incomprehensible, and after a while I stopped listening. Bob Tear, standing behind Cantoris tenors, summed up. "You can tell he's used to running things," he said.

My other wobbly moment was during the Pegy Ashcroft memorial. We had another fine cast: addresses by Harold Pinter and Peter Hall, readings by (among others) Ben Kingsley, Paul Scofield and Donald Sinden, and Judy Dench and Dorothy Tutin in 'Fear no more the heat o' the sun'. The service finished with John Geilgud, who was by then almost ninety, doing 'A lass unparallel'd' from *Antony and Cleopatra*, and 'Our revels now are ended'. I can still hear his intonation of the final words: ' ... and our little life is rounded (pause) with a sleep'.

I was in Devon when Princess Diana died; I heard the news on the car radio. It struck me that we might be needed; we were. The service was on a Saturday; by the Thursday, the day of our first rehearsal, a draft programme was in place. The Receiver General told us later how difficult it was dealing with two families, one of them Royal. It was clear that both the Dean and Neary thought they were in charge - a hint of trouble to come. On the day itself, the most difficult job was done by the young squaddies carrying the coffin, which almost slipped off the catafalque as they lowered it. The strain on their faces showed on the TV film. During the service they relaxed in the cloisters, before doing it again in reverse.

I have a recording of that service; the Purcell *Funeral*

Sentences, to the slow clump of soldiers' boots, still has a frisson. Later, Tony Blair read 1 Corinthians 13 ('Though I speak with the tongues of men and of angels') like a bad actor, and there was Elton John's ghastly *Candle in the wind*. Things picked up for John Tavener's *Song for Athene*, one of his better pieces; it became very popular. The most moving moment was the sight of a small wreath on the coffin, with a card bearing the single word, in Harry's writing, 'Mummy'. The oddest was Earl Spencer's anti-Royal Family speech, and the applause which swept the Abbey afterwards. It was only later that we discovered the rather unusual nature of his own family life. The choir saw less of the service than many; I dared not look out for Pavarotti (say), in case a camera was on me. It was an extraordinary day.

It was also rather profitable; we carpeted our cottage with the various recording fees. But another nice little earner never (for me) came off. The Queen Mother was almost ninety when I went to the Abbey, and her funeral, my colleagues thought, could not be long delayed. We knew, from something which Michael Mayne had let drop, that the ceremonial was occasionally practised in the middle of the night. She came to the Abbey twice in my last term, each time walking from the west door to the east end, though David Dorey, the Dean's verger, had to lead the procession at a snail's pace to accommodate her. She saw me out, and several others, and eventually died about four years after I left.

Perhaps this is the place to explain how we were paid, since it will clarify much of what comes next. The position altered slightly during my time, and some of the detail was Byzantine, but the essence is as follows. For our eight contractual services per week, we were paid a salary. Special services were non-contractual, but payment also came through the Abbey's payroll. A broadcast service would involve a separate fee from the broadcasting organisation (which was why Diana's funeral was so lucrative: there were so many of them). But for certain concerts, tours and recordings we were paid as free-lance musicians, and this money came through the Nearys. To start with, the cheques were printed 'Neary music a/c'; in 1994 this changed to 'Neary Music Limited'. It was, I thought, an administrative detail. Though it turned out to be the crux of the whole affair.

What the Nearys had done was to form a company, Neary Music Limited, to run certain Abbey musical events. They appointed themselves directors and made an annual profit, partly by charging fixing fees for the choir (to which I shall return). They did not tell anyone that they were doing this. In a collegiate body, supposedly based on trust, it was to be their downfall.

In retrospect, the Abbey's dismissal of the Nearys looks almost like a disaster waiting to happen. The Nearys' secretive financial arrangements, the arrival of a new and managing Dean, with a new Canon Treasurer, the sour musical atmosphere ... Someone (never mind who) indiscreetly suggested that the new Dean and Chapter were concerned about musical standards, and were happy enough to jump on any financial peccadillo which they might uncover.

Be that as it may, the first we knew of it was at a Friday rehearsal; the date was March 20th, 1998. No one seemed to be in charge. Then the Organ Scholar, John Hosking, arrived, looking flustered, followed by the Assistant Organist, Stephen le Prevost, who took over; he was clearly under-prepared. The Sub-Organist, Martin Baker, was apparently having trouble with his car. There was no sign of Martin Neary, who indeed never played or conducted in the Abbey again.

The following day (Mendelssohn's *Hear my prayer*), Canon Middleton thanked us for a particularly moving performance. This was unusual; only later did we realise that some sort of statement was being made.

On the Sunday (Lassus' *Missa Bel Amfitrit*), Martin Baker commented on the effectiveness of the suspensions. The following Friday, we heard officially that Neary had been suspended from his duties; his wife, Penny, Secretary to the Organist and Concerts Secretary, was also suspended. On April 30th, the Nearys were dismissed for gross misconduct; Neary appealed to the Queen, as was his right under the Abbey's Elizabethan statutes. The Queen passed the appeal to the Lord Chancellor, who in turn handed it on to Lord Jauncey of Tullichettle, a retired Law Lord. The hearing was held in September. It was not until December 9th that the Nearys' dismissals were finally confirmed.

For all those months, and for two more afterwards, the Nearys continued to live in their Abbey house at 2, Little Cloister. They also attended functions such as the Choir School Fete, as though nothing had happened. ("Have they no shame?" asked an elderly maintenance worker.)

It was a time of uncertainty and strain – and not only for the Nearys. There was the press, for instance. The press, it seems, does not like complex issues; it prefers a hero and a villain, and it quickly made up its mind. The Dean was a bully, and Neary a martyr.

There were a number of reasons for this. The new Dean, Dr. Wesley Carr, had arrived with a somewhat equivocal reputation. While Dean of Bristol, he had sacked both the organist and the head of the Choir School, and there seemed to have been other rows in his past. The current dismissals looked like part of a pattern.

As to Neary, he had always been a networker, and the network now moved into action. The Appeal Fund, to pay his legal expenses, was part of this. But more immediately, the papers were full of letters, interviews and articles, almost all pushing the Neary line. The Nearys, as *The Church Times* eventually noted, were brilliant spin-doctors; meanwhile, the press were very gullible. Alternatively, having decided on their line, they were not going to be swayed by evidence.

I had a small personal experience of this. I was telephoned by a journalist from *The Sunday Times*, Andrew Hall, who asked why the Lay Vicars did not seem to be supporting Neary. I passed him on to John New, as we had all agreed; John is good at being inscrutable. Andrew Hall eventually wrote: 'The dean has a faithful band of followers (including the lay vicars) who can be relied upon to write letters to the press saying … how high morale is at the Abbey.' He does not seem to have asked himself why this was.

Meanwhile *The Times* Diary column was full for months of half-truths, malicious tittle-tattle, and at least one downright lie. (Another way in which the press are gullible is that much of this material is provided by weirdos and malcontents; sensible people mostly keep quiet.) Richard Morrison, an ex-Oxbridge organ scholar, clearly knew what was what, while apparently toeing *The Times* party line. (It was he who, after the result of the appeal was announced, wrote that 'Carr's popularity in the Church of England is about as high as Neary's in the musical profession – i.e., about minus 43 on a scale of one to ten.') A *Guardian* article, notably more balanced than most, contained the following statement from 'a senior figure in church music': 'It is a well known fact that the standard of music at Westminster Abbey is shocking. No one has any respect for Neary. I don't know a single musician who would stand up for him, except John Tavener, who has been heavily promoted by Neary.' These, however, were the exceptions.

And then there was the Diana effect. In years to come, it will no doubt be difficult to recapture the huge emotional shock to the nation of Princess Diana's death, but it was real enough at the time. Her funeral was seen by two billion people, and was widely perceived as a personal and musical triumph for Neary. There was talk of 'Diana's choristers'. It was hard to believe that the man who had apparently master-minded all this could be sacked six months later. It was quite easy to put about that the Dean was jealous of Neary's enormously-heightened profile.

I can write about Neary from a position of strength; I worked with him daily. I necessarily know less about Deans. A Lay Vicar feels the effects of decision-making, administration, and so on, but takes no part in it. For him, a Dean is a little remote.

The previous Dean, Michael Mayne, was described by *The Guardian* as 'an eighteenth-century gentleman'. He seemed to me a bit of a poser, but I got on with him well enough; we had had dealings over the Housman window. One wonders, however, whether eighteenth-century gentlemen always get a great deal done, and I had heard complaints from more than one quarter that issues were not confronted.

Wesley Carr was clearly rather different. He did not have Michael Mayne's presence, and parties and small talk did not seem to be his scene. (It is fair to point out that he arrived with a bad throat infection. I have also been to parties with little voice; it is not comfortable.) I imagine him going through the contracts, the departments, the paperwork, deciding what needed to be done – and doing it. No one in this position is likely to be popular, even when making the right decisions; and perhaps he was not always tactful – or perhaps tact was not one of his priorities. The elderly voluntary guides whose services were dispensed with were certainly rather upset, and possibly with good reason. But the issue of the choir school teachers' pay was instructive. The Dean, as Chairman of Governors, decided that they were being overpaid in comparison with those doing similar work elsewhere, and announced a cut in their salaries. The teachers appealed to their union, who did not support them, but agreed that the Dean was right. The pay-cut, along with the sacking of Neary, was seen in some quarters as an attack on the Abbey's music; the union's position was less widely reported.

As to the Dean's relationship with ourselves, a cynic might say that he ignored us for a year, and then called on our support when he needed it. A realist might say that, having read the files, he was wary of us, and in any case had other priorities. I felt myself that two minutes in the Song School to say hello would not have come amiss.

Meanwhile, life went on. The Lay Vicars as a body decided, at any rate to start with, to keep their heads down, say nothing to anybody, and carry on singing the services. We were, after all, mere pawns; any result was possible, and we all had to live together afterwards. But one was assailed on all sides. Acquaintances who read the papers talked about 'that terrible Dean'. Journalists rang one up. Janet, who sang in the Bach Choir with Penny Neary, was pestered by another choir member who wanted me to write a letter of support to the Nearys. (None of us had done so.) She also sent her love; as she had always looked down her nose at me before, I knew what that was worth. The wife of a cathedral organist told me, as though I was sure to agree, that Martin and Penny could not possibly be guilty. But then I also knew two of the Canons, not well, but well enough to know that they would never have dismissed someone for gross misconduct without good reason, and certainly not merely because the Dean had told them to. These two beliefs cancelled each other out. (In passing, it took a while for the press to distinguish between the Dean, as an individual, and the Dean and Chapter; decisions, of course, were made by the latter.)

And then there were the chorister parents. I have been a chorister parent myself, twice over, and have observed them from more than one angle. Chorister parents as a body are inherently unstable. Their children are usually educated away from home, and have a brief and high-profile life as performers on top of their school existence. They are very young, and the life ends when their voices break. Some chorister parents find this hard to handle, and all are (quite rightly) emotionally involved – too much so to be dispassionate.

In the present instance, the chorister parents came down heavily on the side of the Nearys, which was fair enough; but some of their actions were hardly conducive to harmony. For instance, they threatened to sue the Dean for the choristers' broadcast fees after Diana's funeral; they felt that the Dean should not have given the fees to the Diana Memorial Fund without their consent, particularly as some of them had been put to expense in bringing their children back for the service. They also made sure that the press knew about it. It was pointed out to them that the decision was made at a meeting attended by the head of the choir school and by Neary himself, and that requests for expenses would be sympathetically met – as had always been understood. (The same letter also mentioned that Neary had negotiated with the BBC for an increase in his own fee.) This did not pacify them, however, and the threat to sue rumbled on for a long time.

Chorister parents were active in the Martin Neary Support Group, formed to provide funds for Neary's appeal. In common with my colleagues, I received information about this, with a covering letter from chorister parent Michael Beckett. One of these letters had a couple of pencil notes on the back, which were clearly not meant to be part of the official communication. They read: 'Lay Vicars threatened with dismissal if any contact', and 'Canon Middleton coveting 2, Little Cloister' (the Neary's Abbey house). A subsequent conversation with Penny Neary made it clear that she thought we were forbidden to speak to them, which was not the case. The other item re-surfaced in *The Times* Diary column a fortnight later. I reprint this in its entirety, as it gives the flavour of the times:

> The feuding between the Dean and Master of the Choristers at Westminster Abbey is spilling out of the Chapter House and into the peace and quiet of the cloisters. The wife of an ally of the Dean has been expressing dissatisfaction with her grace and favour home for its lack of a garden. Her complaint comes just as the choirmaster is threatened with eviction from his courtesy abode and its fine garden, after the Dean dismissed him for gross misconduct. Canon Michael Middleton, the Abbey treasurer, and his wife Anne, have lived at No 8 in the Little Cloister, in the shadow of the Abbey, since moving from the Bristol diocese last year. She has been telling friends: "The only problem with our house is that there is no garden."
>
> Middleton used to work for Dr Wesley Carr when he was Dean of Bristol. The treasurer supported Carr, now nicknamed We Slay Choir, during the disciplinary hearing which ruled against Dr Martin Neary, and his wife Penny. The couple deny allegations that they took advantage of their position to further their own financial gain and are appealing to the Queen, who is Visitor of the Abbey,

> a Royal Peculiar under her direct jurisdiction. But if the couple fail, they will have to leave No 2 in the Little Cloister. The house, traditionally the home of one of the Abbey's four Canons, has a wonderful garden with a fabulous view of flying buttresses. A gargoyle at the Abbey says: "The Westminster feud is fast making the eight-year dispute between the Dean and sub-Dean at Lincoln Cathedral look like a Sunday school outing."

Mrs. Middleton replied with great dignity, through *The Times* letter column, that as a clergy spouse she was quite used to living in the house provided, and that in any case arrangements had been made as long ago as the previous August for them to move into a house with a garden, on the retirement of a fellow Canon. The story, in fact, was a blatant and malicious lie. In any case, while an attack on Canon Middleton might be no more than could be expected, an attack on his wife was way below the belt.

It was this sort of manipulation of the press, I felt, which made writing to the Nearys impossible; the most anodyne note of sympathy might have been misused. LAY VICAR SUPPORTS ORGANIST AGAINST BULLYING DEAN ... I could not risk it.

Our own letter to *The Times* had its element of farce. Time had moved on, and I was beginning to form a view. I had witnessed some of the more unscrupulous antics of the Neary faction, and I had both official and unofficial information about the facts of the dispute. A malcontent called Alan Taylor had written an ill-informed letter to *The Church Times* criticising the implementation of the Abbey's 'Restoring the Calm' programme (concerning the control of visitors); four heads of department (Clerk of the Works,

Chief Marshal, Dean's Verger and Chief Cashier) had penned a robust reply. The Dean now suggested to the Lay Vicars that they need not feel bound by their contractual obligation not to contact the media about Abbey matters if, in fact, there was anything we wanted to say. Several of us produced drafts, all of them rather different. There was much stitching and patching. In the end, what we did was to reply to *The Times'* suggestion that the dismissal of the Nearys was symptomatic of a wider attack on cathedral music generally. We testified to the financial and moral support given by the Dean and Chapter to the Abbey's musicians, including the funding of the choristers' education, and we insisted that our morale was high. (It was; I will return to that later.) *The Times* agreed to print it, over our twelve names. In the event, they printed it as coming from Roger Cleverdon alone; Roger was our choir representative. Of course we saw this as an attempt to reduce our impact. (Earlier, *The Times* had apparently 'lost' a letter from Lord Runcie in support of the Dean.) But what amused us was that Roger had contributed nothing to the letter; he was off sick at the time, and had merely agreed to sign what we produced. My own contribution was a semi-colon.

Richard Morrison later described this letter as 'spectacularly disloyal'. Or perhaps we were being loyal to our employers.

All this time the air was full of rumours. Neary had been in financial trouble at Winchester ... Neary had been caught because he had left something on a photocopier ... The Abbey's solicitors had wanted Neary arrested ... The Nearys had wiped their computers ... Neary was going to return for one term, and then resign ... David Hill was going to be the next Abbey organist ... Stephen Cleobury was ... All the best organists had already turned it down (this was long before anyone had been approached) ...

Neary was going to be organist of Guildford Cathedral ... He had applied to Exeter ... He had claimed he would be back by Christmas ... And so on. And there was a recurrent Lay Vicars' nightmare ...

I shall record four other tit-bits from those extraordinary months. Frank Field (the Labour MP and recently-sacked Health Minister) and Dame Ruth Railton (founder of the National Youth Orchestra), regular Abbey worshippers, were reported as complaining about the removal of the communion-rail, which meant that communion had to be taken standing up. Any moderately attentive worshipper knew that this had nothing to do with draconian decisions by the Dean, and everything to do with the fact that (according to the experts) the mediaeval Cosmati pavement in the sanctuary had now to remain uncovered, which meant that those administering the bread and wine could no longer stand on it. The complaint, of course, was in *The Times* Diary column.

Then there was the Great Masonic Plot. I had one colleague who thought that most things were a Masonic Plot. But according to *The Sunday Times* it was Canon Gray (Canon of Westminster and Chaplain to the Speaker of the House of Commons) who approached two peers and claimed that the attacks on the Dean, and the massive tidal wave of support for the Nearys, were all down to Freemasonry. *The Sunday Times* reported a member of Neary's family as saying, "Martin is certainly not a Freemason." In which case it is odd that another colleague reported Neary approaching him in 1997, and asking if he would like to join the Masons.

Thirdly, there was Stephen Darlington's Presidential Address to the Royal College of Organists; he succeeded Neary as President. Neary had been known for some time by the Lay Vicars (and others) as 'Toad'. This arose from certain service papers, the point of which seemed to be to include the words 'Martin Neary' as often as possible. Carol services, for instance: he was Organist and Master of the Choristers, composer, arranger, writer of descants ... and so on. This reminded one colleague of Toad's plans for the banquet after the recapture of Toad Hall:

SPEECH	BY TOAD
ADDRESS	BY TOAD
SONG	BY TOAD
	(*Composed by himself*)

Etc., etc., and concluding:

OTHER COMPOSITIONS BY TOAD

will be sung in the course of the

evening by the ... COMPOSER

Further glee was occasioned by the discovery of the following verse in A.A.Milne's play version, *Toad of Toad Hall*:

The army all saluted
As they marched along the road;
Was it the King? Or Fat-face?
No, it was Mr Toad!

'Fat-face' looked so very much like 'Fart-face'.

Stephen Darlington (from Christ Church, Oxford) quoted a different verse:

The clever men at Oxford
Know all there is to be knowed,
But they none of them know half so much
As intelligent Mr Toad!

Having mentioned a few of Toad's drawbacks, he commented that 'he did have some admirable qualities, such as extraordinary tenacity and endless optimism.' (This was just before the hearing.) A few lines later, he suggested that 'I suspect I should leave this subject rather quickly before I get into deep water.'

I would not like to speculate on the extent to which Stephen Darlington knew what he was doing. But it all seemed too good to be true.

And finally, there was the Hymn Album. At about the same time as the 'Toad' speech, Sony brought out a double CD of hymns, with Neary conducting the Abbey choir. Half of these we had done for another company; presumably Sony had bought them in. With the hearing only a few days away, it was a magnificent piece of timing. The album, which was much played on Classic FM, was called *Perfect Peace*.

And so to the hearing. We had more than one meeting with the Abbey's solicitors, and were asked for witness statements. I wondered about the propriety of appearing for one side and not the other, but was assured that there was 'no property in witnesses'. In any case, all they wanted was a few facts; I would have provided facts for whoever asked. The main ones were that I had no knowledge that Penny Neary was charging fixing fees, and that no letter had appeared in the Song School announcing the formation of Neary Music Limited; the Nearys had claimed the opposite. In the event, fixing fees were to be a crucial element of the hearing.

A fixer engages musicians for recordings or concerts; he usually takes 10-15% of their fees. But it had struck all of us that there was a difference between engaging random freelance musicians and engaging a standing salaried choir such as ourselves. There was no record of a cathedral organist charging fixing fees for his own choir. In any case, whose choir was it?

The hearing was held in private; I was relieved not to be called to it.

When Lord Jauncey's Determination was finally published, it was unequivocal.

> For some three and a half years (he concluded) Dr and Mrs Neary ran a business whose principal earning assets were the lay vicars and the choristers. They derived profits from this business in the shape of fixing fees and surpluses on events involving the choir. They did not tell anybody in the Abbey what they were doing. They disclosed to no one that they and not the Abbey authorities were entering into some contracts on behalf of the choir. The fact that the Abbey authorities had all the information which would have enabled them to find out about the contracts, had they been so minded, does not alter the position. Dr Neary sought an increase in salary for Mrs Neary without mentioning that she was already receiving substantial sums by way of fixing fees. Both Dr and Mrs Neary, when the existence of the separate account became known to the auditor, indicated that it was an imprest account without going on to mention its other purposes. By these activities and their silence during this long period they were in clear breach of their duty of fidelity to the Abbey. They used their position as Organist and Music Department Secretary to make secret profits over a long period and they entirely failed to inform the Abbey authorities of what they were doing, notwithstanding the fact that there were ample

> opportunities so to do and no good reason for not doing so. I consider that this conduct was such as fatally undermined the relationship of trust and confidence which should have subsisted between them and the Abbey …
>
> For the foregoing reasons I shall humbly report to Her Majesty my determination that the Dean and Chapter were justified in summarily dismissing Dr and Mrs Neary.
>
> *(Lord Jauncey's Determination, pp.49-51)*

On the matter of fixing fees, Lord Jauncey had earlier written:

> There was however dispute as to whether any role existed for a fixer in relation to a salaried choir … Both Mr Tipping and Mr Nixon were firmly of the view that there was no room for fixing a salaried choir when the numbers needed and available for any event could be determined with ease on the premises. Mr Nixon who had sung in a number of choirs explained that ad hoc choirs composed of freelance singers would usually be administered and booked by a fixer but in the case of standing choirs such as that at the Abbey, St Pauls and Westminster Cathedral the administration of the choir for the event would be done by a salaried member of staff with no additional fixing fees being payable. There was before me a witness statement of Mr Simon Preston, Dr Neary's immediate predecessor as organist at the Abbey, who stated that in 20 years experience as an organist in Cathedrals he had never heard of a Cathedral organist taking a fixing fee for participating in

> events such as concerts, tours or recording ... I have no hesitation in accepting the evidence of Messrs Tipping and Nixon that in general there is no room for fixing a salaried choir. There is necessarily a considerable difference between the work of assembling from scratch and then organising a group of freelance singers who may be widely scattered and that of simply ascertaining the availability of a stated number of salaried singers who are all under the existing management. More importantly prior to 1994 ... no fixing fee was charged by or paid to the Abbey in respect of third party promoted events in which the choir took part. The administration for such events was carried out by Dr and Mrs Neary as part of their salaried duties. I therefore conclude that the need to fix the choir and charge percentage fixing fees therefor neither accorded with the prior practice at the Abbey nor with the usual practice in similar ecclesiastical institutions. (pp.24-26)

Lord Jauncey was rightly scornful of Neary's claim that, prior to 1994, his conducting fees had included a 'notional fixing fee'. Indeed, the whole business of fixing fees seems only to have arisen because of a suggestion made by Sony in 1994: "And will there be the usual 10% management fee?", to which the Nearys had agreed. An example of the way it worked was our Britten recording, made for Sony in 1996. Penny Neary booked the twelve Lay Vicars by leaving notes in the Song School; she also booked Martin Baker, the Sub-Organist. Later, she distributed cheques. For this she received rather more than twice what a Lay Vicar got for doing three three-hour sessions.

Lord Jauncey also pointed out a number of anomalies. Neary had claimed that the fixing fee was at most 15%;

but sometimes it was more. The Nearys admitted that on two occasions they had charged fixing fees for the choristers, which even they now agreed was wrong. The scale of fees was random, once as low as 4%. On the choir tour to Moscow, according to Lord Jauncey, much of what Mrs Neary claimed as fixing work overlapped with duties for which she was paid by the Abbey as Music Secretary. Of our three Barbican concerts in 1995, '96 and '97, fixing fees were charged for the first two, but not the third, when (in Lord Jauncey's words) 'more information was being required by the Dean and Chapter as to the finances of the music department'. (pp.33-34)

As to the total figures, Lord Jauncey reported that 'Between 6th April 1994 and December 1996 Mrs Neary received fixing fees ... to an amount exceeding £11,900 in addition to her salary as Organist's secretary and concert secretary, She also received a dividend of £1,500 from Neary Music Limited in lieu of fixing fees during 1997'.

However, the Abbey authorities did not emerge unscathed. Their attempt 'to convene a disciplinary hearing at such short notice and without a detailed statement of the case being made against the Nearys must score gamma minus on the scale of natural justice' (p.48). Lord Jauncey also noted 'the apparent lack of interest in the Abbey as to what was going on'. He concluded: 'I find it surprising that neither the Precentor ... nor the Dean asked Dr Neary directly about the fund and its operation as soon as they were aware of its existence. Had they done so and had the parties been prepared to discuss openly and frankly the Abbey's concerns, to acknowledge that serious mistakes had been made and to consider the reasons therefor, it might perhaps have been possible to avoid the present unhappy situation with all its attendant publicity and to have reached a rather less dramatic resolution of their differences.' (p.52)

The press, most of which had expected a different outcome, seized on Lord Jauncey's criticisms of the Abbey. A *Times* leader referred to 'a disastrous, pointless scandal' and more or less suggested that the Dean ought to resign. *The Independent*, under a headline 'Dean censured for "callous" sacking', did not mention the main verdict until paragraph three. Early editions of *The Evening Standard* told the story as they thought it ought to have happened. *The Sunday Times*, which had been virulently anti-Dean, did not refer to the sacking at all.

But the traffic was not all one way. Jenni Murray, in *The Express*, under the headline 'Time to face the music over Abbey fiddle', told Penny Neary to stop bleating, and concluded, 'The Dean's only crime seems to have been to have joined an organisation late in 1997 that had, as the judge pointed out, been administered badly in the past and endeavour to run its affairs in a more professional, open and honest manner.' (This was an important point: one of the Dean and Chapter's problems of public perception was that failures of oversight had occurred under the previous Dean and Canon Treasurer, whom the present administration felt unable to criticise.) Andrew Brown, in *The Church Times*, wrote of the Nearys' 'extraordinary powers of self-belief and persuasion of others in the teeth of the evidence'; this was under the headline 'Psst! Wesley won.' He also wrote, 'If it had been someone working for me who had done what the Nearys did, I would have sacked them as soon as I found out; I would have felt that they had improperly acquired £10,000. Had they excused their actions, as Lord Jauncey suggested the Nearys did, on the grounds that I should have noticed what was going on, I'd have paused for a moment of speechless goggling and then sacked them twice as hard.' And it was he who pointed out the following from the Jauncey Determination:

> In a memorandum submitted by Dr Neary for the Disciplinary Hearing he stated that Mrs Neary had had responsibility for the book-keeping of the company and in respect of her own trading as a fixer. He (i.e. Neary) continued: "I cannot be held responsible for any mistakes or errors which she may have made" (p.46).

Lord Jauncey's comment was: 'I am not impressed by this ground' – a remarkably restrained reaction, as Andrew Brown noted. Chris Tipping (a married man) said that it made his blood run cold.

Pro-Neary and anti-Dean letters, protests and petitions continued for a long time, both in and out of the press. As late as July, 2000, there was still a nutter writing poison-pen letters, and claiming the moral high ground while doing so. Weary of talking about it, I got my version down to one sentence: "A man was dismissed for gross misconduct, appealed, and was found guilty as charged."

My own feeling about the verdict was principally one of relief – firstly, that it was all over; secondly, that the Nearys were not coming back, which would by this time have become musically and personally impossible; and thirdly, that what I in time had come to see as the 'right' side had won. Though in another sense no one won except the lawyers, who were reputed to have cleared almost half a million pounds.

As to the Nearys, I felt sorry for them in the sense that one would feel sorry for anyone whom one had known for a long time and who had got themselves into such a mess. Certainly they were unwise in their financial dealings; possibly they were naïve. Perhaps they were badly advised. (Their accountant did not appear at the hearing, which is interesting.) But that was hardly the whole of it. A *Times* leader claimed that they were not fraudsters but 'an unworldly couple who drifted into a business arrangement with only the haziest notion of what they were about.' No one who knows the Nearys could think that they were unworldly. *The Church Times* was more accurate: 'Dr Neary is known to be ambitious,' they wrote, and quoted his critics as saying that he is 'a good politician but not a great musician'. Neary's rise was fuelled by ambition, networking and various sorts of hard work, as much as by any great musical talent; and his downfall was caused, to all appearances, by greed. A witness statement reputedly contained the sentence: 'Dr Neary is an egoist who lives in a dream world and has no concept of him ever being wrong.' There is some truth in this; certainly, it was the impression given by the post-verdict interviews. There was further acrimony, seized on by the press, over the terms under which the Nearys were to leave the Abbey; but for Neary to ask to be made Organist Emeritus, while simultaneously being sacked for gross misconduct, was patently absurd. I had sometimes tried to persuade sceptics that inside Neary was a nice man trying to get out. They had both been kind to me personally. I could, in one sense, feel sorry for them. But I cannot think that they got any more than they deserved.

I could not help reflecting, too, on how the whole experience had drawn people together; apart from the lunatic fringe and the chorister parents, the Abbey community was united in a way that I had never known it before. Janet was told by a Canon's wife that it had been dreadful – but that it had been worth it.

And finally, as a footnote, I was impressed by the dryness and clear-sightedness of the law. The Neary faction had almost given the impression that they would romp home on the back of their own publicity, spin-doctoring and anti-Abbey wrecking tactics. On the other hand there were those, I felt, who thought that Neary ought to lose because he was, in their view, a poor musician and an unpopular man. To Lord Jauncey, quite rightly, none of this was relevant.

And what had been going on musically all this time?

The immediate effect of the suspension was that Martin Baker, the Sub-Organist, became Acting Organist and Master of the Choristers, a position he was to hold for almost two years.

I remember Martin's audition for the Sub-Organist's job. The other two short-listed candidates were good musicians in their way; but the organ buffs in the choir preferred Martin's playing. What struck me was his conducting; he appeared to be doing very little, but the music came quietly up through him, and made itself felt.

On arrival, he remained quiet, and just got on with it. After only a few days, he had to accompany Elgar's *The Spirit of the Lord*. It was very impressive – beautifully orchestrated, harp-ripples and all. We thought we were onto a winner.

And then we discovered his improvisation, which was to be the wonder of the next eight years: virtuosic, inventive, harmonically fascinating (very French) and often extremely witty. He once told me that it was best if you disengaged the brain and let the feet and fingers do it. John Nixon, who has black and white views, described him to me later as 'practically a genius'.

He was not really all that quiet, or at any rate, he had the sort of quiet arrogance of someone who was well aware of his talents. You do not have to make a lot of noise if you know you are good. I think he thought Neary was a fool.

There was also a hooligan undergraduate inside him – and no doubt still is. One day, Neary insisted that the curtain across the organ screen should be open at all times. Martin thought this unnecessary, as they already had excellent contact through a TV monitor. He retaliated (at the Communion) by improvising with his hands on the keys and his head well below them, meanwhile calling out pedal notes to the Organ Scholar, John Hosking, who played them with his hands. The visual effect to those below was of an organ being played by nobody.

His previous conducting had been intermittent; now we discovered what he could do. The effect was immediate. All sorts of nonsense disappeared. Tempos were suddenly utterly musical (if, for my taste, sometimes a little fast). The boys were made to sing lines and phrases. Music was real music again – and rehearsals were real rehearsals. The repertoire broadened; for years, it seemed as though we had only done thirty-seven pieces. The Psalter changed, week by week and month by month. All around me, colleagues whom I had thought of as terminally disillusioned seemed to be rediscovering the joy of it all. It was, I felt, a resurrection experience.

Of course it took a little time to take full effect; old habits die hard, particularly in children. But it was this *re-invention* of the choir that I found so fascinating. Martin never acted like a caretaker; from the first, he was determined to mould the choir in his own image. Standards in all things were important – processions, for instance. His conducting was utterly unshowy; he once said that when the boys strayed rhythmically, he *reduced* the size of his beat, to make them watch. And yet one knew just what he wanted, and it was all very compelling. The suggestion of a smile at the end of a piece meant everything. To command this absolute attention while not apparently exuding obvious charisma was, I thought, very clever. And all the time there was a part of him that was slightly above it all – as if (perhaps) he was in touch with an ideal version, which mere mortals could never give him. I am sure that this element of detachment was part of his strength.

For a term and a half, the organists were short-staffed; fortunately, John Hosking was able to take much of the strain. In September, Philip Scriven arrived as Acting Sub-Organist. Philip was a great asset. He, too, knew how pieces ought to go, and his performances were often quite different from Martin's. (Some of my copies had to have two sets of markings.) He soon took over most of the men's voice services, and searched the library for new repertoire. Much of what he came up with was rather ordinary, but the change was refreshing. Perhaps he talked too much; he spoke sense, but did not always watch the clock. I remember several evensongs where the music was entirely new; the first third would be thoroughly rehearsed, the second third would be skimped through, and the rest we only saw in the service. It was all great fun. He and Martin, while never wasting a moment, occasionally fooled around like a couple of kids. They were, in fact, either side of thirty. We were all delighted for Philip when he got the Assistant's job at Winchester Cathedral.

Once it became clear that Neary was not returning, the question of his successor arose. The Abbey appointed head-hunters, for which they were criticised. (At that time they would have been criticised for more or less anything.) The defence of the head-hunter system is that the man eventually appointed would never have thought of applying if he had not been approached. The process took another six months.

My own position was clear. Martin had taken over the job in very difficult circumstances, and had made a huge success of it. Of course he was young, but no one was suggesting that he should continue until he was sixty-five;

the Abbey, in common with the rest of the world, had by this time heard of fixed-term contracts. Not to appoint him, I thought, would be a kick in the teeth.

The head-hunters consulted widely; it was also open to anyone to approach them. I was unable to attend their meeting with the Lay Vicars, but I telephoned and gave them my views. I also pestered one of the Canons. The only person who would not help them was Sir David Willcocks; he made it clear (on a radio programme) that he was used to advising Deans and Chapters, and that talking to mere head-hunters was beneath him.

When James O'Donnell's appointment was finally announced, there was a huge sense of sadness on Martin's account. One of my colleagues told the Dean that he was "bitterly disappointed". The same colleague told me later: "I've been here for twenty-seven years. First of all we had old Doug, and everyone moaned about him. Then we had Preston and the balloon went up and people moaned about him. Then we got the biggest plonker in the world. Finally we've got someone we actually like, and they go and appoint somebody else."

A few weeks later, on the last Sunday of term, Martin improvised on the *Te Deum* after Eucharist. It was excruciatingly loud, and unbelievably exciting; he was getting something out of his system. Canon Harvey complained to me that members of the congregation had left with their hands over their ears. "Of course, it's a very fine improvisation," he said, in his beautifully modulated voice, "but I wonder if the same effect might have been achieved with a little less violence."

I: Of course, he's a very young man.

Canon H: I wonder if the Abbey is quite the right place for him to do his growing up in. (Pause.) Still, we shall never really know if we made the right decision.

(I recorded these conversations at the time.)

Of course, the feeling on Martin's behalf was in no sense a feeling against James. James had an excellent and well-earned reputation, having done great things at Westminster Cathedral, which was just down the road. Many of us knew him, and had worked with him. He was a first class musician, and a good man. It was clearly a very sound appointment. (The papers fussed about his being a Roman Catholic – but then so was Martin.)

And gradually one's perceptions altered; like the chorister parents, I had been emotionally involved, and detachment was hardly likely. Martin's music-making had always had an element of spontaneity, risk, and downright mischief. Could one absolutely trust him, on a Royal occasion, say, not to improvise on *God save the Queen*, without adding a bit of *Pop goes the weasel* as well? Of course it would be very tastefully done ... He once tickled me, and annoyed Neary, by playing as a voluntary E.H.Lemare's *Moonlight and roses* – after an all-Purcell evensong. I could not quite bring myself to agree with Canon Harvey, but in time I began to see what he meant.

And the situation changed. The biggest and most delightful change was that Martin was appointed to James' vacant post at Westminster Cathedral. He told me later that he had taken a long time making up his mind; everyone thought he ought to apply, but he wanted it to be his own decision. He also said that the Abbey job would have carried a lot of baggage with it; as it was, he could take his Abbey experience with him, and start afresh.

In due course, the Assistant Organist at Westminster Cathedral, Andrew Reid, became Sub-Organist of the Abbey, and the Abbey's Acting Sub-Organist (by this time it was Robert Quinney) moved down the road in what looked like another job-swap. Martin and James had each got their own man. Over a year, James was able to appoint three new Lay Vicars. The storms were over. Perhaps the right men were in the right places. The good times were beginning.

But by then I was not there to see it. Voices age in different ways. My own problem was that the top of the voice, which had never been remarkable, now seemed to be declining at the rate of about a semitone a year. In theory, and given a contract renewal, I could have gone on until 2001, when I would have been sixty. In practice, I knew I ought to stop before then, and it became a question of timing. It would have been fun to have done two more terms, and seen James in, but in fact I think I got it about right. I announced firmly in October, 1998, that I would retire at the end of the summer; and I stuck to it.

I had a good send-off. It began with the Dean presenting me to the Queen after a Special Service. I have a nice photograph of this; the Queen, the Duke of Edinburgh, the Dean and I are all smiling. ("Surely your voice isn't breaking again?" the Duke asked.) The Dean and Chapter held a party for departing musicians in St Catherine's Garden. The Dean had sent a note regretting that he could not be present; in the event he arrived, late, but in time. I was touched that he should have made the effort.

I had persuaded Martin to let me write a piece to mark my departure. When this turned into a pair of pieces, he did not blink, but put them both down for my penultimate week. (Song, by Toad ...) This was also my last verse week (*Purcell in G minor, Jehovah*). And in due course, my last service (Howells *St Paul's, I was glad*), and the end. I had been a Lay Vicar for just over nine years. I felt very privileged, and in spite of everything, I had had a lovely time.

And now there is peace at the Abbey. True, two members of the congregation still stand when the choir processes out, and ostentatiously sit down again when the Dean and Chapter do so. True, one or two newspapers are still looking for trouble. But the music is in good hands, and the musicians are getting on with each other, and with the Dean and Chapter, for the first time (I imagine) since the days of Edward the Confessor.

And of course I miss it dreadfully. There were the difficult times, and the dailiness could get one down; but in another sense it is the dailiness that I miss. Putting on a cassock, being in the middle of it all …

There was the buzz of one's regular verse weeks. On my last Easter Sunday we did the Mozart *Coronation Mass*, with a section of the English Chamber Orchestra; I have sung as a soloist with the ECO. I remember the satisfaction of getting through the rather Gerontius-like solos in Elgar's *Seek him that maketh the seven stars*, at the end of a long Sunday. There were old stand-bys: the verse in the Byrd *Second Service*, or Howells' *Coll.Reg. Nunc Dimittis*, which I did often. Or little things: 'O bear your tribulation like a rose' from the *Hymn to St Cecilia* (that Pears-like diminuendo on the last note), or the end of E.W.Naylor's *Vox Dicentis*. (Dan Norman, a tenor thirty years my junior, once told me I had given the definitive performance of this, which touched me.)

And then there was a whole range of pieces which were not only wonderful but which I found physically satisfying to sing: either tenor part of the Tallis *Lamentations*, for instance, or Byrd's *Civitas sancti tui* (*'Jerusalem desolata est'*), or Taverner's *Dum transisset*. Or little moments like the Amen in the Howells *Gloucester Nunc*, that scale down from the F sharp, leaning on the E sharp as one went …

And somehow, most of all, I miss the psalms. It is difficult to say why. Sometimes they went by in one's sleep, like motorway driving, and one woke up to wonder where the last ten verses had gone. But a perfect match of chant and psalm, with a conductor who understands words, is hard to beat. That Goss chant in E, with the parts overlapping, to 'The Lord is my shepherd' ... Reciting on the top E ...

Two years after I left, I sang with the Vasaris in Canterbury Cathedral. It was 'By the waters of Babylon', to that C.H.Lloyd chant in G flat. (A single chant: how can you make magic out of ten chords?) I was so upset I thought I would have to go out. I decided I had better not do this sort of thing again.

My life as a singer is nearly over (see Chapter Eleven). Poetry gave me up; I gave up teaching. While I am still composing, I am still alive.

Ten

COMPOSING

POETS EXPECT to be self-taught; composers, on the whole, do not. My first piece of any size, *Mater Dei*, was programmed at its second performance with a piece by Nicola Lefanu. She was not only the daughter of a composer, Elizabeth Maconchy, but had studied with Egon Wellesz and Goffredo Petrassi, and was currently lecturing in composition at King's College, London. All of which was rather intimidating; what, after all, had I done? It was only later that I took to writing firmly, 'He is self-taught'.

I have described my beginnings at prep school. I continued to fiddle around with it at Uppingham, though in no very systematic way, and with little encouragement. In my last year, I put on a trio movement (clarinet, violin, cello) at a Paul David concert.

Cambridge seemed full of clever people, and I was not reading music anyway. I wrote a few solo songs, two little part songs which Noel Osborne's group performed, a pair of easy organ pieces which I published years later for the amateur market (they sound like bad Warlock), and the Responses.

David Willcocks had begun a series of annual competitions to write a piece for the King's choir; in my first year, it was for a *Jubilate*. I had a go at this and came fifth; the winner was Simon Preston (*Preston in C*). Jonathan Harvey (*in F*) was runner-up. Years later, Jonathan told me how impressed he was that David had taken his undergraduate piece so seriously. In my second year, the task was a set of Responses. There came a day when I would either finish these, or go on a punt; the punt nearly won. I was surprised and delighted to come first, emotions which seemed to be shared by David himself. In my third year we broadcast them. Interest was shown. David was in charge of Oxford University Press's church music section, and OUP published them. It was at a time when everyone did the various Tudor Responses, but there seemed to be no other modern ones except the Bernard Rose. They have sold very well for forty years, and, largely through broadcasting royalties, have been my most lucrative piece. They also, irritatingly, are what I am best known for.

I never really capitalised on this success; I did not know how to. I wrote quite a lot of music in our early married years, including a set of songs to Chinese poems which I did on honeymoon, but I had no outlet for them; they were not *for* anyone. From the age of about twenty-seven, I began putting my creative energy into poetry. I never thought of myself as a composer; I just wrote pieces from time to time. But I increasingly thought of myself as a poet.

I started again by accident. In the winter of 1977-78, Peter Godfrey took over King's College choir for two terms while Philip Ledger was on sabbatical; Jonathan was in his last year as a chorister. At a party after Advent Carols, Peter mentioned my Responses, and wondered whether I would consider doing a men's voice *Mag and Nunc*. Why not, I thought, and wrote him my *F sharp* service. F sharp is a lovely key, but awkward to write in; you are constantly on the edge of enharmonic change. In other ways, too, I could have made it easier for the singers. But it is not a bad piece in its way. Peter Godfrey did it once; Philip never took it up on his return. But I had a piece which had been done by King's, and I felt it ought to be marketable.

OUP and others sent it back, and eventually I tried Oecumuse, about whom I knew nothing except their rather brash publicity. Barry Brunton replied by return of post, full of enthusiasm and eager to publish anything else I had; he knew my name from the Responses. I shall say more about Barry later; in the meantime, I seemed to have a publisher.

I wrote a *Jubilate* for Winchester (not very good), and another *a capella Mag and Nunc* which I wished on Richard Seal at Salisbury, though it was not really suited to his choir; he had only six men, and there was too much *divisi*. Then I moved to Guildford. Philip Moore, as a composer himself, was encouraging; indeed, I first met him when I discovered he was putting on the *F sharp* service. He introduced the *Salisbury* service, and a little anthem (*Before the ending of the day*) which I wrote for Marc Rochester at Londonderry, and commissioned a piece for the Diocesan Choirs Festival. It was about this time that I added a Lord's Prayer to my Responses, at the insistence of Michael Barry ('Self'), the Guildford alto. Andrew Millington, Philip's successor, was equally supportive; I wrote him two anthems with organ, *In the beginning* for ATB, and *I look for the Lord* for full choir.

My organ writing was simple and mostly chordal at this stage, though some of the chords were interesting (I always liked chords); my mastery of organ writing, such as it was, came later. As to choral writing, as a singer I ought to have known how to do this, and in many ways I did. But because King's choir could sing anything, and Winchester also did a lot of modern music, I thought that I could write anything, and that people would sing it. It was Guildford, not a specially good sight-reading choir, which taught me the need to be practical. What was wanted, except for special occasions, was interesting new music which could be rehearsed in the comparatively short time available. I learnt my craft slowly; I was fortunate to be allowed to do it on the job.

It was also at Guildford that I met Andy Phillips, who sang as a tenor deputy. Andy was extraordinary. He did some solo work, sounding a little as though he might be rather good if he gave up brandy and cigars; he taught at Wellington school; he ran a concert agency, and a hire music library; he directed a comedy quartet called the Demon Barbers; he fixed orchestras for choral concerts, and he conducted two choirs. He was perpetually busy – he never took a holiday – but he always seemed very laid back. Soon he was commissioning a carol for one choir, and a half-hour unaccompanied choral piece for the other. The latter was terrifying; I had never written anything longer than a five-minute *Mag and Nunc.* But I beat him down to fifteen minutes, and wrote *Mater Dei*; you can write a long piece, I discovered, by stitching shorter ones together. There are five movements; one of the texts is my own. It is a little short-winded, particularly the *Magnificat* with alternate plainsong verses, but it has some attractive music and I still rather like it.

Over the years, I wrote for his choirs *Lux hominum*, an unaccompanied piece in three movements which the BBC has just broadcast; *Beati mortui* (double choir, in memory of my father); *Ecce tu pulchra es,* words from the Song of Solomon, for choir and a rather luscious mezzo, Jenevora Williams, who gave me some lessons when I went to the Abbey; and *Tombeau*, which I shall describe later. Having premiered a piece with one choir, Andy would then do it with the other, and several years later it would probably crop up again. He also did pieces not specifically written for him, including the next big piece I was to write.

When I moved to Chelsea, Ian Curror was equally good. For him I did a setting of the Collect for the Royal Hospital, in which I managed to give each of the twelve singers a small solo phrase. Chelsea caused me to think about sopranos. I did a lovely little setting of *The Lord is my shepherd* for Jean Carter and the choir, and a sensuous *By the waters of Babylon* for Jean and Margaret Crossland; we did them as introits. Ian also took on items from the Oecumuse catalogue.

It was at Chelsea Royal Hospital that I came across the Vasari Singers. The Vasaris had been founded in 1980 by a group of LSO Chorus members who wanted something smaller; they met in Julia Field's back room (Julia sang at Chelsea). After a year, the conductor left, and Jeremy Backhouse, singing bass, offered to take over; twenty-odd years later he is still doing it, having conducted several other choirs simultaneously in the meantime, including (occasionally) the BBC Singers. He is currently chorus master of the Guildford Philharmonic, and recently conducted Mahler's Eighth ('Symphony of a Thousand') in Guildford Cathedral.

The Vasaris have similarly gone from strength to strength. With no organisation except what Julia provided, and still seeming like a few friends having fun, they won the Sainsbury's Choir of the Year Competition in 1988. Time has caught up with them a little; they are now a charity, there is a proper committee (Janet was secretary for three years), but there is still the same friendly atmosphere, and the same lovely blend.

Because there was overlap between Chelsea and Vasari, I wrote them a little piece (*Round me falls the night*), and a slightly bigger one (*Incarnation*) for their Christmas Eve midnight mass in Westminster Abbey; they subsequently sang it in an early round of the Sainsbury's competition. It was soon after this that Julia asked me what I was planning next. Rather diffidently, I admitted that I had thought of a *Requiem*. "If you write it," she said, "we'll do it." It seemed at the time one of the most generous things ever said to me. It still does.

A *Requiem* was the biggest thing I could think of. There was the competition: Victoria, Mozart, Berlioz, Verdi, Fauré, Duruflé. There was the text: one was looking death in the face... One morning I woke up knowing how it started, so I pitched in. I wrote it in two weeks of an Easter holiday, and the first half of a busy summer term. It is for unaccompanied choir, with two soloists. There was always going to be a soprano, but since Julia has a big, dramatic mezzo, I wrote a part for her as well. The piece seemed huge while I was writing it, but in fact it is a miniaturist's *Requiem*; I should have given myself more space. The first performance was in Canterbury Cathedral; not everything was perfect, but the thing definitely existed.

I have written further pieces for the Vasaris. For a complete Clucas evensong in Canterbury, I provided a double choir *Mag and Nunc* and a rather intense anthem, *My God, my God*. There were two further concert works: a *Stabat Mater* with string quartet ("I thought of trying choir and strings, but I've never done it." "Why not string quartet?" said Jeremy), and *Songs of Farewell*, for choir and piano – about the saddest music I have ever written. My latest piece for them, *Rorate coeli*, I wrote as one of a group of five composers commissioned to celebrate the choir's twenty-first birthday; the others were Diana Burrell, Roxanna Panufnik, Bob Chilcott and Howard Goodall. I had the best seat in the house, next to the lovely Roxanna. "Beautiful," she breathed, as my piece ended.

For the last twenty years or so, the production line has

been pretty constant. I cannot describe every piece; I am merely taking a survey.

In 1992, the Vasaris made a complete Clucas CD; it was to contain the *Requiem, Mater Dei, Lux hominum, My God, my God* – and the *Stabat Mater*. Jeremy, who still sometimes thought like an amateur, had booked a quartet for the premiere consisting of people he happened to know. They were just about adequate apart from the cellist, who was hopeless. I persuaded him to sack her for the recording, but her replacement was not much better. The record company (Cala) deleted the piece on the grounds of inadequate string playing.

In other ways, circumstances were against us. The church, which we used because it was free, was unresonant. Too many of the singers could not make all the rehearsals. We were recording in the country at the height of summer – and poor Julia Field has hay fever. The other soloist failed to come to rehearsals, did not know her part in the *Requiem*, and was only intermittently in tune. The same thing happened when she did it for Ian Curror at the Royal Hospital. I found this unforgivable; I thought I deserved better. Humphrey Carpenter's Britten biography tells how Britten would suddenly, and rather cruelly, drop performers he had lost interest in; I knew how he felt. I was glad that the recording was out, and some of the singing was good; but it was not the Vasaris on top form.

My second choral recording, made in 1998, was rather different. Andy had wanted to do a CD for years, and had once nearly got it together, but in the end I could see that it would only happen if I put some money in. This galvanised Andy; he suggested Laudibus, the National Youth Chamber Choir, who were on the books of his Chameleon Arts Management, with their charismatic conductor, Mike Brewer. I love young voices; they blend better. We used the recording studios at Guildford University. Jeremy Backhouse produced. The recording company was Upbeat, run by a pushy lady called Liz Biddle.

The earlier recording seemed to have sunk without trace, though I discovered later that it was still in the catalogue, so I decided to repeat the *Requiem*, since I thought it could be popular. The other pieces were the *Stabat Mater*, a rather minimalist *Crucifixus*, my *Shakespeare Songs* (written for a Shakespeare birthday concert), the *Songs of Farewell*, and *Sinfonia Sacra*. The latter was a large unaccompanied piece in four movements, partly put together from existing material; the recording constitutes its first performance.

The singers arrived on a Friday evening, from all parts of the compass, never having seen the music; they did a twelve-hour day on the Saturday, and by Sunday tea-time the job was done. In many ways one had the best of both worlds; these youngsters were entirely professional, but with all the energy of youth, and a total disregard for anything like union rules. By the end, I was an emotional wreck; I felt like the drowning man whose whole life was going past him. If the choir had really known the music, they might have been more inside it; nevertheless, the results were first-class, and were greatly helped by some expert technical work. Brian Kay played the *Shakespeare Songs* on his BBC Radio Three Sunday morning programme, and for several months Classic FM featured two movements from the *Requiem*. The CD never quite took off, but it had been worth doing.

Over the course of my time at the Abbey, my attitude had become more professional; I was now a full-time musician, and composing was part of my free-lance work. Of the larger pieces written during the Abbey years, I ought also to mention *Miserere*, a setting of Psalm 51 for choir and organ, commissioned by Richard Stangroom's Banstead Musical Society, and a heavy revision of *Remember, O Lord* for twenty voices, originally written in 1984 to commemorate the four hundredth anniversary of the death of Thomas Tallis; it uses half the forces of Tallis's *Spem in alium*.

But much of what I wrote was liturgical. It was good to write for the Abbey choir, though it took time to persuade Neary that this was an option. One day we did *Wood in E Te Deum*, men's voices. "Boring piece," I said, as we went out. "Yes," he replied, "why don't you write us a better one?" Two years later, he asked me to add a *Jubilate*. I was busy with the Housman book at the time, so I partly recycled it from a bit of *Lux hominum*. Then it was a *Benedicite*. The earlier pieces were unaccompanied; this was with organ. I put in some twiddles for the birds of the air, a snatch of Debussy's *Nuages* for the clouds, some broken glass noises for the ice and snow, moos for the cattle – and so on, and also the odd inaudible joke for the organist: a contra-bass cuckoo, for instance. We did it twice; I do not think it has been revived since. There were further men only pieces, including a verse anthem (*Miserere mei*) for four tenors and organ, with alto and bass chorus, one of a number of unique pieces I seem to have written. It was planned so that John Nixon had the last word. At the start of the *Te Deum*, I had marked the second tenor part (John's) 'slightly prominent'; one may as well play to one's strengths.

I enjoyed writing for men's voices; it is a specialised skill. Also, there was a shortage of good modern men only music, and I was, I hoped, filling a gap. After I left the Abbey, I completed my *Westminster* service by doing a *Mag and Nunc* (with organ) for James O'Donnell. There are also some men's voices Responses (for Guildford), written, by a happy chance, forty years to the month after my earlier set.

But I also wrote for the full Abbey choir. Soon after I left, James commissioned a series of ten introits; they are mostly in eight parts, and rather romantic. Then there was my week as Master of the Queen's Music. After Malcolm Williamson died, Chris Tipping told me that I ought to succeed him, and that he was organising a march on London in my support. Later the same day, James O'Donnell rang: would I like to write two little antiphons for a special service? It turned out to be the Queen dedicating a memorial to holders of the Victoria and George Crosses; the Archbishop of Canterbury, Rowan Williams, preached.

I find I have written pieces of one sort or another for Chichester, Exeter, Guildford, Liverpool, Ripon, Salisbury Southwark and Winchester Cathedrals, Southwell and York Minster, Westminster and Paisley Abbey, and King's College, Cambridge. Some of these pieces are fairly non-prestigious, or were written for special occasions only, or have dropped out of the repertoire; but they keep me in touch with the cathedral world.

I have written twice for choir and orchestra; each piece lasts about twelve minutes. *Evening Hymns* was for Jeremy Backhouse's BBC Club Choir, which sounds grander than it is; the singers are BBC staff – producers, scene-shifters. I used a standard small orchestra: strings, single woodwind, one horn. What made me think I could orchestrate I have no idea, but I kept things simple. The text was an anthology of my own devising (I like doing these): verse one of 'The duteous day now closeth', (a Brahmsian double canon at the ninth), the 'Evening Hymn of Charles I', Samuel Daniel's 'Care-charmer sleep', and Newman's 'Lead, kindly light'. It is a delicious piece, which

I loved hearing at both its performances. Alas, I have no recording.

Tombeau was an Andy Phillips commission. I knew the sound I wanted: strings, horn and piano. Andy, always accommodating, agreed. I set 'Fear no more the heat o' the sun': rich string writing, horn counter-melodies, piano-ripples. But before the choir comes in, there is a brief and brisk sonata-form movement, some of whose motifs recur later. It is my comment on the dramatic situation in *Cymbeline*: two young men sing the Dirge over the body of a third – but the third young man is really a girl, who is not dead at all. I am not sure that any other setting recognises this.

There is also an orchestral version of *Songs of Farewell*; Andy put it on. But I prefer the piano version; it is a question of scale. In any case, only Ravel can orchestrate piano music so that it sounds as if it were orchestral all along.

I have been lucky in my organists; I have written for some distinguished players. I began with some little Hymn Preludes, just to see how it went. Ian Curror did them at St Stephen Wallbrook, and Robert Crowley came across the programme; he wondered if I had any more organ music in me. Thus began a long association.

Robert has commissioned pieces from all sorts of people over the years: Alan Bush, Humphrey Searle, John Gardner, Alan Ridout, Francis Jackson. My first piece for Robert was based on *Christe, qui lux es*, a tune which has obsessed me; I also use it at the end of *Lux hominum*. He soon asked for another, and I wrote *Credo*, based on the plainsong intonation, which he premiered at King's. In due course, I showed these to Martin Baker; then I wrote him a piece of his own. My *Suite* has five movements, each based on plainsong; apart from the *Requiem*, it was the longest piece I had written. The Abbey premiere was one of the great days of my life. A little later, I wrote an organ duet, *Ballade*, as a wedding present for Martin and his fiancée, Anne-Elise Smoot.

The following year I did a piece for Peter Wright, who was by now organist of Southwark Cathedral. I listened to a lot of organ symphonies, with the intention of writing one – but it turned out too slight; I did not have that sort of stamina. So I called it *Sinfonietta*.

I thought I had done with organ music for a while, but Robert was keen for more, so I wrote him a rather angry *Passacaglia*, which also incorporates the Coventry Carol, and *Diversions on 'London New'*, mischievous and bitonal. A few years later, he suggested a *Toccata*, so I wrote him a jolly one. About the same time I did a big and exciting piece (*Urbs beata*) for John Scott Whiteley, assistant organist at York; John premiered it in the Minster, rather splendidly.

Finally (ignoring some lesser things) there is the *Organ Symphony*, for solo organ; Robert thought I ought to write one, and it seemed (in 2002) time to have a go. The problem was structure; it had to last at least twenty minutes to justify its title. I decided to start with a standard sonata-form movement – (varied) exposition repeat, development section, and so on. The *Scherzo*, also in sonata form, introduces the B.A.C.H. theme, which appears first as the bass of a slightly frivolous waltz. The *Finale*, a set of variations on the Passion chorale, concludes with a section which incorporates the chorale, B.A.C.H., and bits of the other movements. The whole thing is an act of *hubris*; it has also given me more trouble than anything else I have written. Robert seems pleased with it; I have yet to hear it.

For some time he, too, had wanted to do a recording. We had a false start with Harry Mudd, who had done good work in his day, but was by now reduced to taking money for recordings he was no longer allowed to make. It ended in the small claims court. Robert eventually got it together with Lammas, who specialise in choral and organ recordings; we used the organ of St Alban's Cathedral. Robert played really well – he is very thorough – and the editing was expert. Now he wants to record the Symphony. People like him, and Andy, and Jeremy, are worth their weight in gold.

I have given the impression that I write mainly for choir and organ, and within the cathedral orbit generally, and by and large this is true. But I have done other things. English cathedral composers find it hard to escape the influence of Howells, and perhaps they ought to. Other influences are mainly French: Fauré, Poulenc, Duruflé. In my Poulenc phase, I wrote several wind sonatinas; one of them, for clarinet, is published by Lengnick. I have written a unique Housman song cycle: the only one specifically for counter-tenor (Simon Gay), the only one which starts with a waltz and ends (for good scholarly reasons) with a Bach chorale, and the only one which sets A.E.H.'s 'We'll to the woods no more' next to the French poem it derives from. And I have written several works for double bass.

I met David Heyes after one of Andy's concerts. David is a bass player, a teacher (at Wells Cathedral School), arranger of conferences (forty amateur bass players with professional tuition – that sort of thing), commissioner and publisher of double bass music, and enthusiast for all things bass. He told me that there was a lot of bass music, mostly written by bass players, and that he was trying to persuade composers to join in. I did him a little *Suite* of six pieces; some of them are now on the Trinity College of Music syllabus. Soon he wanted something bigger. A sonata? A concerto? Why, when there were more interesting instruments to write for? So I did a *Te Deum* for choir and four double basses; Andy Phillips put it on. Next I wrote *Serenade*, for soprano and bass quartet (Mrs David Heyes is a soprano). I used the two verses of *O mistress mine* as book-ends to words from *The Merchant of Venice*. It had a lovely performance from David's international bass quartet (principals from the Danish National Orchestra, the Rotterdam Philharmonic, and so on). What particularly pleased me was that the players liked it. Finally, I wrote him a little *Sonatina*.

Below the top level, a lot of things are kept going by mad enthusiasts – people like David. Barry Brunton, of Oecumuse, is madder than most. He began with a choir in Bishops Stortford; it did a lot of new music, which he also published. Then he took them on tour to the States. His backer pulled out half way, the boys were sent home (it was a mixed top line of sopranos and trebles), and the bailiffs met him at the airport. But he kept on publishing. In the early days it was all photocopied manuscript, or occasionally Letraset; later, computer typesetting came in. But he kept to his principle of producing a master copy, and only running off sets as they were ordered; it saved storage space. Another principle was that nothing should go out of print – admirable, but in some ways a pity; there are early pieces of mine I would like to see the back of. His catalogue is vast: a lot of reprints (Stanford, Victorian stuff), and much of the rest of rather limited value. His publicity is frequent and verbose, and (I imagine) much ignored. But he has published yards of my stuff over the years; some pieces sell, and it is all there if anyone wants it.

An advantage of small publishers is that you can ring them up for a chat at odd moments. I particularly enjoy my chats with Adrian Self, of animus (sic). Adrian is an organist, and a compulsive composer, who worked for OUP for a while before setting up on his own. His catalogue is much smaller than Barry's, and he is far more selective, though I have occasionally persuaded him to go against his instinct if I had a piece which I thought might sell – my *Westminster Mag and Nunc*, for instance, of which I unloaded quite a few by the simple expedient of sending inspection copies to cathedral organists. It grieves him to have to turn down good music because it is uncommercial; what does sell, he tells me, is 'easy-peasy' stuff for high voices. He certainly did rather well with a little carol of mine, *In the dark time* (words by Peter Dale: new carol texts are hard to come by, and I was glad to have this one). Adrian seems very unworldly; I think his wife handles the money.

I can count nine publishers altogether, which is too many. And some more statistics: I have eight surviving settings of the Evening Canticles, and over fifty carols and anthems – also too many. Three-quarters of this material is published. I would particularly stand by the Westminster *Te Deum*, *In the dark time*, and *There is no rose* (for Chichester), and of the anthems, *Te lucis ante terminum* and *Rorate coeli*. I am also rather fond of some of the Westminster introits (unpublished).

There is a view, held mainly by academics, or by singers who think they are academics, that one should not compose at the piano. But there are voices on the other side. Stravinsky, a Rimsky-Korsakov pupil, enquired about this. "Some do, some don't," was the gist of Rimsky's reply, "and you probably will." (He did.) Or Ravel: "Of course I compose at the piano; how, otherwise, does one discover new chords?" Or a rather lesser composer, Francis Jackson, who (John Scott Whiteley told me) said that whenever he wrote something away from the piano, the first thing he wanted to do was to try it out – so why not start there? I use it less than I did. I like to do structure away from the keyboard, which is more useful for working out detail. This is particularly true of organ music; I need to try it under the fingers to make sure it is practical. And sometimes the fingers discover what the brain would not have thought of.

I love going to rehearsals, and working with performers generally. I particularly enjoy amateur choirs; I get excited, and start to take over. I have no conducting technique, but I persuade myself that, since I wrote the piece, anything I do must be authentic. I also know exactly what I am able to expect from singers; an orchestra would be a different matter.

With organists, it is largely a matter of registration; they know more than I do, but I have the sounds in my head. Sometimes a performer's view is different from one's own. Robert recorded the last of my *Plainsong Preludes* much faster than I had indicated, but it seemed to work, so I let him.

I find composing a mixture of excitement and stress. Starting a piece is exciting; then the stress builds up, and I sleep less and less. Some pieces are also more important than others. The third element is hard work; if you put the hours in, you get the thing done. I start after breakfast, and work through till lunchtime, having planned for an hour or so while lying in bed. Sometimes I wonder why I do it; the world takes fairly little notice, and why don't I just sit in the sun? But I would get bored; and besides, it is endlessly fascinating. I think I am just beginning to learn how to do it.

I go through phases: my minimalist phase, my austere phase (mostly choral – particularly *My God, my God*). Last year (2001-02 – years go from September to July), I wrote nothing but doodles: two parish choir anthems, a baroque set of variations for recorder quartet, some sight-reading tests for Trinity College, London, a book of easy manuals-only pieces (which taught me things: I had never written imitation Bach before).

Then I had had enough of doodles. This year I was going to write nothing at all, or something huge: hence the *Organ Symphony*. It is an over-the-top piece, and now I am thinking in terms of neo-classical restraint. We shall see.

I do not like writing about my pieces; if they are any good, they will stand up for themselves.

Eleven

BIN-ENDS

THE FIRST time I went into Durham Cathedral, a visiting choir was doing my Lord's Prayer; between the rehearsal and the service I made myself known to the conductor. A year later, I was in Durham again, and mentioned this. "I'm glad to know the end of that story," said someone. "Our conductor came into the vestry and told us there was a nutter outside claiming to be Humphrey Clucas."

Once the four of us – Janet, Jonathan, Tristram and I – sang at a friend's wedding. Tristram was an ageing treble, Jonathan a youthful baritone (later he turned tenor). The boys and I did solo items, and the four of us sang Mozart's *Ave verum*. The organist was Catherine Ennis, whom none of us knew; she was a little suspicious. Tristram was due to sing the *Pie Jesu* from the Fauré *Requiem*; Cathy put down the B flat chord and said, as to a very small child, "One, two, three, *four*!" Tristram looked at her. "Actually," he said, "I take it a little slower than that." After which things went fine.

On an Abbey tour, I found myself in the Handelhaus at Halle. They send you round with a taped commentary, and musical excerpts. In one room, a tenor was doing an aria from *Acis*. Roger Cleverdon turned to John Buttrey. "That's you!" he said. It was. The recording was twenty years old, and made with the Deller Consort.

A grotesque moment: James Lancelot playing the big chord before the final chorus in *Blessed be the God and Father*, full, organ, in St John the Divine, New York. There was a cricket-pitch length between Decani and Cantoris. Aurally and spatially, we were overwhelmed. "It was like playing a jumbo jet," said James.

Once I had a letter in *The Times*. 'Sir,' I wrote, 'I am interested to learn from *Holiday Which* (report, March 9) that St Paul's Cathedral fails the test as a tourist attraction. I write to point out that it has a little-known secondary use as a place of worship.'

One hears odd things at cricket matches; people talk as though the row in front were deaf. Edward Wickham and I once discussed the Great Neary Crisis, which may have amused somebody. At a Test Match, I sat by a married couple; he was watching the cricket, she was nagging away about this and that, and otherwise doing crosswords. "It's something to do with Shakespeare," she said. "Is there a word 'orisons'?" I could not resist it: "Nymph, in thy orisons be all my sins remembered," I told her. I wondered if I could make it the only thing I said all day – and I did.

At Ravensbourne, I taught a boy who did not seem to do any homework. He was pale and weedy, and what he did manage was covered in blots. It was time to get heavy. "What do you mean by this?" I said. "After my dad died," he quivered, "my mum cries a lot, and I have to sit with her." I could not think of a reply.

My mother told me how bored she had been by Virgil's *Georgics* (all those bees), and how they used to play up the Latin teacher. Old Aunt Mary says she was called Miss Housman: could this have been a relation? I have done readings with the late Stephen Housman, who *was* a relation, though only through A.E.H.'s stepmother (a cousin, also called Housman).

Mother's description of playing hockey: standing around in the cold and being hacked on the shins by Mary.

If I put everything in, the book becomes a rag-bag; if I leave things out, they are lost for ever ...

I have seen my mother kiss my father on the lips when he was an incontinent old man with his teeth out. They were married for fifty-seven years.

I am fascinated by the areas where my various interests coincide. In July, 2002 I attended a memorial service in Southwark Cathedral for Ben Hollioake, the Surrey and England cricketer, who was killed in a car crash. It was a clash of cultures. On a very hot day, young sportsmen stood about in wraparound shades; when they entered the cathedral, they pushed them up on their foreheads as they do on the cricket field. The choir sang *How lovely are thy dwellings.* A verger with a silver wand led the lesson-reader to the lectern; it was Alec Stewart. He read Henry Scott Holland's 'Death is nothing at all. I have only slipped away into the next room ...', not getting all the emphases quite right, but with great natural dignity. Mark Butcher, another Surrey and England colleague, sang a specially-written song to his own guitar; he has one of those light high-tenor pop singer's voices which break into falsetto at the top.

The song had shape, and was competently done. Adam Hollioake, Ben's brother, gave an address – long, and very emotional; he could hardly get through it. All around me, tough-looking sports people suddenly found they had something in their eye. After Diana's, it was the most tear-jerking service of this sort I have ever been to. Ben was very young, and even as spectators we felt that we knew him.

In the Abbey, I did memorial services for Brian Johnstone and Denis Compton. Rodney Williams, who knows nothing about cricket, was impressed by the way that E.W.Swanton read the lesson; Swanton was over ninety. J.J.Warr told a Winter of Discontent story. "What do you think of this new three-day week, then, Denis?" "I'm not working an extra day for anyone." David Gower sat opposite; I had last seen him in Antigua. He had the room above mine, and his baby kept me awake.

Soon after I arrived at the Abbey, the Hardy Society held a service in Poets' Corner; it was to celebrate the one hundred and fiftieth anniversary of his birth. They wanted 'The Choirmaster's Burial' from Britten's *Winter Words*; when they found that a real tenor would cost real money, they lowered their sights and hired me. I was a member of the Society at the time, though no one seems to have made this connection. I sang within a few feet of Hardy's grave; Neary accompanied on the Abbey's inadequate upright. Flowers were brought from Max Gate, and a folk fiddler played Hardy's violin.

Once I put on a poetry reading in the Jerusalem Chamber. Michael Mayne organised a series of these, sometimes by quite distinguished people; once a year he put on Chapter Choice, by himself and the four canons. Why not Lay Vicars' Choice, I thought, as I passed their publicity notice. Within five minutes I had recruited Andrew Giles, because he has literary interests, and

Lawrence Wallington because he is outgoing. (Later, it emerged that he had done performances of *Façade*.) Each item had a connection with music. We did Wyatt's 'My lute awake', 'The Unquiet Grave' (a ballad), A.E.H.'s 'Is my team ploughing?' (well-known through song-settings), 'The Choirmaster's Burial' (again), Gurney's 'Bach and the Sentry' and 'The Old City (Gloucester)' – read by Andrew (a Gloucestershire man), a lovely poem by the Australian Gwen Harwood called 'David's Harp' (the hymn tune) – and so on. We began with a snatch of *Romeo and Juliet*: three musicians are discussing why music has a 'silver sound'. "What say you, James Soundpost?" "Faith, I know not what to say." "O, I cry you mercy; you are the singer." No point asking the singer – he's thick; it is the original thick-singer joke. We also did something (I forget what) by Sylvia Townsend Warner – novelist, short story writer, and in odd snatches rather a good poet. In early life she had helped to edit the old Tudor Church Music volumes, and we still occasionally sang from tatty copies 'edited by E.H.Fellowes and S.Townsend Warner'.

Once in a second hand bookshop I found *The Escaping Club* by A.J.Evans; it was sitting on top of an unsorted heap. The bookseller described it as a rare example of First World War prison-camp escape literature (there is plenty from the Second); I knew of it because Evans had played a single Test against Australia in 1921. Evans describes travelling through German villages at night, and having to be wary of barking dogs and their rattling chains. The poor protagonist of Schubert's *Winterreise* has the same problem; in '*Im dorfe*' you can hear the dogs in the pianist's left hand. Before I read Evans, I had taken this for a poetic conceit. Similarly, I had always thought of the Biblical sheep and goats as mere pastoral metaphor; yet when I went to Israel, there they were, still herded together by day and separated at night.

❖

One afternoon in Canterbury, I was discussing sermons with the Vasaris; I had often thought I would like to give one. "Come and do it at our place," said Jane Beeson; "we have all sorts of odd people." (Pause.) "We had Anne Widdecombe once." Her place was St Michael's, Cornhill. It never happened, partly because Jane moved to Lincolnshire. But I thought about it.

It was to do with music and worship. One thing which works like the *B Minor Mass* give us is a sense of the sublime. The *Et in terra pax* fugue, for instance: the tune creeps in so quietly, but with a huge and utter confidence in what it describes; and then the semi-quavers start, and the counterpoint; and the thing is an enormous dance. Here, staggeringly, is a fully realised angelic vision of peace on earth. Or the *Sanctus* – the angels praising God. A sublunary echo, no doubt, but an inkling.

Another thing they do is strengthen our faith; one cannot possibly listen to the *B Minor*, or *Spem in alium*, or look at Chartres Cathedral, and imagine that these things are based on a delusion. Rationally, they might be; but one's whole being cries out against it.

Small masterpieces will do: Purcell's *Hear my prayer*, for instance – eight-part counterpoint, every line intense and meaningful. There was an accidental in the second tenor part which could go one of two ways; John Nixon and I would try either, depending on our mood. Both were perfect. I used to watch with delight how Purcell overlaps the two bass parts in *My beloved spake*; he does the same with altos towards the end of the *B flat* Evening Service. Little things. God is in the detail

There was lots more. I was going to finish by suggesting

that any choir singer knows the action of the Holy Spirit. I have never heard church musicians discuss this; mostly, they just get on with it. Instead, there are leg-pulls, in-jokes, badinage. Once every ten months or so, every cathedral choir I have ever been in gets a fit of the giggles (most reprehensible, not conducive to worship). Somehow this is all part of it.

A few months ago, Nellie Mason died. Nellie worked in the greenhouse at Red Trees, the home of my paternal grandparents. The greenhouse was vast – perhaps forty yards long – and Archie (grandfather) had all sorts of things going on there; at one time he was trying to grow tobacco. As quite small boys, Stuart and I used to spend a few days at Red Trees every holiday, and would go to see Nellie; she soon discovered that I could sing, and singing in the greenhouse – hymns, carols – became a feature of our visits. She herself sang in a local church choir.

I forgot about Nellie for forty years or so, until my Aunt Mary told me she was still alive – so I wrote. She was well over ninety, and not up to replying, but her daughter told me that she was delighted by my letter, and particularly impressed that I had sung at Diana's funeral. She must have been the first church musician I ever met.

I did not in the end give up singing entirely when I left the Abbey. To begin with, I worshipped with Janet at St Dunstan's in Cheam – an 8 a.m. said Eucharist, Book of Common Prayer. One day, singing a hymn somewhere, I thought what a pleasant sensation this was; three quarters of the voice still worked perfectly well. I also thought that I ought to be doing something for my new church; then the penny dropped, and I joined the choir.

It was not in a good state. St Dunstan's was perpetually looking back to what it perceived as its glorious past: full choir stalls, a big anthem each week, and a succession of rather good organists, one of whom, Barry Wordsworth, currently conducts ballet at Covent Garden. Now they were down to a handful of children, a rather silent contralto, and quite a good bass who soon re-located to Birmingham. I was the only tenor – "though the assistant organist sometimes sings tenor, when she isn't playing the organ". The organist himself was amiable enough, but had no fire in his belly; children do not flock to church choirs any more, you have to go and find them.

I did what I could for a year, and then transferred to St Alban's, a daughter church, smaller, and much more lively. You could not quite say that the organist, Roger Brice, was a good musician, but he is an enthusiast and a notably good organiser, and, young himself, he attracts young people. The choir is more than twenty strong, and of all ages from seven to seventy-eight. Everyone talks to everybody – a change from St Dunstan's.

I shall sing for a little longer. I like the camaraderie; I like putting on a cassock and feeling the church year go round me. But the voice is in terminal decline, and the physical pleasure it gave has almost gone.

When my mother died, we came into some money, and decided to buy a holiday property in Devon. We wanted a bolt-hole – one up and one down would do. We ended up with Tor Cottage, Coldridge – three bedrooms, Grade II listed, and thatched. I did not intend to be involved with the village; I wanted to be a recluse. But this, too, did not work out. There was little in Coldridge except a part-time post office (since closed down) and a small mediaeval church. As well as Sunday services, they have Compline on a Wednesday. We got to know people; Janet started doing the flowers. I became a relief organist (anyone who can get through a hymn is an organist there). I published some easy manuals-only pieces – *The Coldridge Organ Book*. We found we were part of the village.

We spend a few days there each month, and several weeks in the summer. By chance, two ex-Abbey men, Chris Tipping and Roger Cleverdon, have houses nearby.

But we shall not retire there; it is inconvenient for the old. Shops, doctors, hospitals, one's children, are all too distant. It is a *jeu d'esprit*. When the time comes, we shall sell it.

I find that I have named two people – my father and my first headmaster – as slightly disappointed men. Perhaps most of us are. Nothing we do is as it ought to be. Creative folk, too, seldom receive the recognition they hope for, or think they deserve. I have had plenty in a modest way, but no one ever said, "Hats off, gentlemen, a genius." I should not have believed them if they had.

And yet I can truly say, with my father, that it has been a lovely life. I have never been poor, or uncomfortable, or seriously ill. I have a loving and supportive wife and two dear sons. I have pushed some minor talents a very long way. I have lost God, and found him.

Of course there are regrets, for things done and undone. If there is a purgatory, I will surely go there. (I naively imagine that each church service I sing lets me off a little.) And yet in the end, I believe I shall meet my loved ones, and that those whom I leave behind will join us. There will be music, and I shall be part of it. And when that happens, I shall have come home.